Other Work by Tom Baker

The Sound of One Horse Dancing
Full Frontal: To Make a Long Story Short

PAPERWHITE NARCISSUS

TOM BAKER

iUniverse®

PAPERWHITE NARCISSUS

Cover artwork and design by Steve Jakobson
Author portrait by Don Bachardy

iUniverse books may be ordered through booksellers or by contacting:

iUniverse
1663 Liberty Drive
Bloomington, IN 47403
www.iuniverse.com
1-800-Authors (1-800-288-4677)

ISBN: 978-1-4917-5142-8 (sc)
ISBN: 978-1-4917-5143-5 (hc)
ISBN: 978-1-4917-5141-1 (e)

Library of Congress Control Number: 2014918742

Printed in the United States of America.

iUniverse rev. date: 10/31/2014

For
Allan-Michael Brown

He who meets his going double
must go himself.

—old German proverb

It was a great mistake, my being born a man,
I would have been much more successful as a sea gull or a fish. As
it is, I will always be a stranger who never feels at home, who does not
really want and is not really wanted, who can never belong, who must
always be a little in love with death.

—Eugene O'Neill, *Long Day's Journey into Night*, act 4

CHAPTER 1

Funerals are not an unusual occurrence in Arlington National Cemetery, but today there was something different about the cortege as it marched somberly up the hillside to its final destination. The black Cadillac hearse led a small procession of six pallbearers: three noncommissioned officers in full dress uniform representing the army and three from the navy, followed by the US Marine Corps band. It was an impressive display of military pomp, creating an eerie tapestry against the manicured hillside dotted evenly with rows of white stone markers—eerie because there were no mourners following the small formal procession. It was just three years ago that the world had watched in disbelief as President Kennedy was laid to rest on the hillside not far from where Tim was now standing.

The terse announcement in the *Times* had indicated that internment would be private. There had been no calling hours at the Frank E. Campbell Funeral Chapel on Madison Avenue, where the body had been laid out. In lieu of flowers, donations to the Actors Fund were suggested. The only public homage was the solemn High Mass officiated by Cardinal Spellman the day before at St. Patrick's Cathedral. The pews off the main aisle had been filled with men and women in military uniform, nuns and priests, students from Catholic University and Yale Drama School, and many well-known faces from the entertainment, media, and political worlds. Fifth Avenue had not been blocked with so many chauffeured limousines since the funeral of Stanley Strafilino, the Mafia kingpin who'd been pumped full of bullets while eating a plate of scungilli at Umberto's Clam House on Mulberry Street in 1957.

Tim waited in silence a few feet away from the tarpaulin covering the mound of dirt that would soon seal the coffin and its contents. He'd been waiting over an hour, pacing back and forth among the rows of markers, reading the names of strangers buried there, sobered by the fact that many of them had not lived to be as old as he was now.

The sun was glaring brightly, suggesting like a cruel joke that it would be a balmy spring day in the nation's capital, rather than the first day of December with snowflakes on the ground by evening. The increasing dampness in the air puffed off the Potomac in restless gushes as Tim brushed back the shock of light brown hair that perpetually hung down over his forehead. The black Cadillac hearse sagged to a stop on the gravel roadway. The small procession halted silently behind, waiting as the uniformed driver slowly opened the rear compartment door. On cue, the six NCO pallbearers marched forward and gently slid the flag-draped coffin out of the car.

Tim felt self-conscious and a little silly holding the clump of white narcissus he'd cut in his aunt's greenhouse before leaving for the cemetery. Red's favorite flower, Paperwhite Narcissus, would be the only nonmilitary farewell she would receive.

The pallbearers moved forward slowly, gently setting the coffin on the taut canvas straps stretched across the mouth of the open grave. The Marine Corps band drew up in formation a few yards to the left and stood in stony silence.

Tim winced as he saw the familiar black silhouette of Father Hartwell emerge from the passenger side of the hearse. The Jesuit had accompanied the body from New York and was now approaching the gravesite to recite final prayers. Hartwell had assisted Cardinal Spellman at yesterday's requiem Mass in St. Patrick's Cathedral, and even though the elderly cardinal had wanted to complete the ceremony at Arlington, his health was too fragile to risk the arduous trip down the New Jersey Turnpike.

The cardinal and Red had shared a long and somewhat unconventional relationship. She'd first met the famous New York archbishop when her older brother, Ben, introduced them at a Saint Vincent De Paul Friends of the Poor fundraiser at Tavern on the Green. The venerable clergyman was the guest speaker, and Ben was his unofficial escort, a function he frequently performed since the archbishop's staff assistant was often indisposed by his recurring spells of asthma. At the time, Ben was a chorus boy in the original Broadway production of *One Touch of Venus* by Kurt Weill and Ogden Nash, starring Mary Martin. Ben and the cardinal, it was widely suspected but never confirmed, were having an affair. The archbishop, the soap opera actress, and her chorus boy brother had become a familiar threesome on the New York social scene, regularly appearing on the society pages of the *Times* and *Women's Wear Daily*.

After the Mass in New York, Father Hartwell had to return to Washington, where he taught at Georgetown, so he was the logical person to perform the final rites. The priest nodded to Tim, who diverted his eyes to the silver coffin, avoiding further exchange with the Jesuit. It would be unavoidable later. The stems of the fresh clump of Paperwhite Narcissus were becoming slimy—verdant tears seeping through his clenched fist.

Tim had met Red when he was sixteen years old. He first saw her playing Cleopatra in a production of *Antony and Cleopatra* at the Olney Theatre in Maryland; Tim's junior class from Fairfield Prep attended a performance of the Shakespearean classic as part of the "arts in action" program established by a wealthy alumnus. Tim was mesmerized by the voluptuous actress whose brilliant red hair cascaded like a wild cataract down her back to just below her waist. The performance Tim attended with his classmates was a Wednesday matinee in June. The following week, when classes were out from Prep for the summer, Tim went to stay with his aunt Blade at her home on Thirty-Third Street in Georgetown. This was a tradition that had started when Tim was in first grade and that would continue through his college days at William and Mary. Tim's parents were happy to ship their son off to his doting aunt for the first month of summer vacation before he would return to Westport for a caddying job at the Longshore Country Club.

That summer after his junior year at Fairfield Prep, Tim moved into Blade's townhouse and took over the basement apartment, with its separate entrance from a back alley, where he parked his aging VW. The "cave," as he affectionately called the apartment, opened onto the patio and greenhouse, where he spent hours cultivating orchids, roses, and his favorite, Paperwhite Narcissus.

From the cave, he would drive the battered VW out to Olney Theatre in Montgomery County to see his sensuous goddess perform the role of the ill-fated Egyptian queen. Tim went to every matinee performance for three weeks.

It wasn't until the final performance of the run, a Sunday matinee in mid-June, and the seventh time Tim had seen Cleopatra die from the asp bite, that he waited while the audience vacated the auditorium. He stood in the lobby with a bouquet of white narcissus he'd brought for his heroine. Tim asked one of the ushers picking up discarded programs if she would take the flowers backstage to the actress. Instead, the girl gave the shy young man a suggestive wink and directed Tim around back to the stage door entrance. Before he realized what was happening, he was being escorted down a long hallway cluttered with racks of costumes and into Cleopatra's dressing room.

"Miss Ryder … you have a visitor," the flirtatious usher announced, leaving Tim blushing awkwardly within the intimacy of the dressing room.

Red took a long drag on the cigarette cradled in her right hand, gave a quick visual appraisal of her young visitor, smiled warmly, and exhaled a cloud of smoke sensuously. She nibbled off a tip of tobacco on her middle finger.

"Well there, a gentleman caller," Red said with a smile, offering a limp, delicate, unfolded hand.

"Hello, Miss Ryder," Tim said politely. "It's a pleasure to meet you. My name is Tim, Tim Halladay." He proceeded to tell the actress how much he had enjoyed her performance. Red invited him to sit as she casually peeled off her spiderlike false eyelashes and dabbed Albolene with a Kleenex on her face to wipe off the greasy stage makeup.

"So, kid, what makes you so interested in Shakespeare?" the actress inquired as she lit another cigarette and took a deep drag, puffing smoke into the stale air of the dressing room.

Tim told her that he was in the drama club at Fairfield Prep, where he was a junior, and that he had been in several school plays, although they were pretty limited, since the Jesuits would allow only plays with all-male casts. The previous year Tim had played a small role in *Twelve Angry Men*. He told Red he also took dance classes, despite his parents' objections, and had done a few shows with the Westport Community Theatre.

"You know, I live in Westport," Red said unexpectedly. "When I'm not the Queen of the Nile, I commute to the city to tape *Another World*."

"I knew you were on TV," Tim acknowledged, "but I don't get to see the program."

"I hope not," Red laughed. "The Jesuits would hardly approve of your watching soap operas in the afternoon."

"I've seen *Antony and Cleopatra* seven times in the past few weeks," Tim confided. "You are the most amazing actress I've ever seen onstage—even better than Kim Stanley."

"How old are you, Tim?" Red asked, studying the young boy sitting in her dressing room.

"I'll be seventeen next month," Tim replied, trying to appear mature.

"Of course," Red said wistfully. "Of course …" The actress drifted off. Her son would have been just Tim's age. She had been doing Laura in an Actors Studio workshop production of *The Glass Menagerie* when she had the miscarriage.

"And the flowers?" Red asked, accepting the bouquet and cupping the white narcissus in her hand, closing her eyes to inhale their hypnotic fragrance.

"I force them in my aunt's greenhouse. I grow them all year round. Just kind of a hobby. I know … it sounds corny. But I like to watch them grow out of the pebbles and bloom."

"Narcissus are my favorite," Red said, brushing Tim's cheek with her hand and gently kissing him, leaving a big red lipstick smudge on his face from her stage makeup.

Red's real name, and the one she used onstage, was Sarah Ryder, but she said she had always hated the name, even as a little girl. Her mother had named her Sarah because it meant "princess," but growing up, she had been much too wild and tomboyish to feel like a princess. It was her father who had first started calling her Red, and the name had stayed with her: all her friends called her Red.

"Do you really think anyone would take seriously an actress named Red Ryder playing Cleopatra?" They both laughed at the absurdity, a laughter they would share many times again, a laughter Red would never share with her unborn son.

"Dearest brothers, let us faithfully and lovingly remember our sister, whom God has taken from the trials of this world …" The drone of the priest's words dragged Tim back into the present time. The coldness of the prayer seemed a trite tribute to such a glorious lady. As the final words were mechanically read by the priest, Tim felt only an empty numbness.

"… may unite her with the company of angels in heaven. Through Christ our Lord in heaven. Amen." Father Hartwell made the sign of the cross with his right hand over the coffin, the gesture disappearing forever into the damp morning air. And then the priest continued the final words of the service. Tim's lips moved by rote, but no sound came out.

"Eternal rest grant unto her, oh Lord. And let perpetual light shine upon her. May she rest in peace. Amen."

There was a slight pause as the grim gathering stood by silently, and then in one dismissive breath, Father Hartwell concluded the service. "May her soul and the souls of all the faithfully departed through the mercy of God rest in peace. Amen."

Father Hartwell folded closed the small black book from which he'd read, signaling the end of the service. An awkward pause elapsed before the Marine Corps band raised their instruments in unison and played "Amazing Grace." The notes drifted sadly over the peaceful setting as two of the NCO pallbearers, with the precision of robots, retrieved the flag from atop the coffin, folded it into a triangle, and presented it, by default, to Father Hartwell.

The soldiers in the band returned to rigid attention as they finished the hymn, and then after a full minute of silence, the bugle player raised the shiny brass instrument to play the familiar call to rest. The mournful sharp notes of "Taps" echoed above the hillside and evaporated over the winding Potomac. When the bugler had finished, he returned to the formation, and on cue, the soldiers briskly marched away from the site and back to the gravel roadway. They moved with purpose, as if having finished this obligation, they were now off to the next assignment. The six NCO pallbearers who had delivered their precious cargo to its final destination followed several paces behind.

Father Hartwell approached Tim, who'd been standing in the same spot, still holding the bunch of fragrant white flowers. "It's hard to accept," the priest said, his voice trailing off. "She was a remarkable woman."

"Yes," Tim said flatly.

"She was very proud of you, Tim," Father Hartwell offered, placing his hand on Tim's shoulder.

"Red was a real mentor … always supportive," Tim said, fighting back tears.

"I know," the priest said as if to himself. "Do you mind if I ride back with you?"

"Sure, of course," Tim responded automatically.

"Somehow going back to the university in a hearse leaves me a bit cool," he said with a small smile. "Let me tell the driver to go on."

While Father Hartwell walked toward the roadway where the driver was waiting by the parked limousine, Tim hesitantly approached the abandoned coffin still suspended over the open grave. He gently touched the cold metal surface with his right hand. A barrage of images whirled in his mind: the hours he'd spent in Red's acting workshop at the White Barn Theatre; the Sunday mornings he'd ridden his bicycle to her cottage at Compo Beach to hang out with her actor and writer friends who gathered every week for coffee and doughnuts; the telegram she'd sent him from Kuala Lumpur on the opening night of *Our Town*.

Tim placed the delicate white flowers on top of the coffin and turned away. He joined Father Hartwell, who was standing on the roadway with his back to the gravesite.

"I'm parked just down the bottom of the hill," Tim said, motioning, and the two walked slowly without speaking toward Tim's ten-year-old VW Beetle. It wasn't until they were inside the car and approaching the main gate of the cemetery that Father Hartwell spoke again.

"God, that was rough," the priest commented.

"Yes," Tim agreed quietly. "The last two days have been pretty heavy."

"Were you in New York yesterday?" the priest asked.

"Of course," Tim answered, irritated by the question.

"Oh ... I didn't see you," the priest said, "but of course there must have been five hundred people at the Mass."

"More than that," Tim assured him. "Lots more than that."

The beat-up VW chugged into the traffic circle outside the cemetery and wound around to the entrance of Key Bridge.

"Are you up for lunch, Tim? Or rather, what about a drink first?" the priest offered.

"Sure, why not," Tim didn't want to carry his hostility toward the Jesuit any further. It was inevitable that the two would continue to cross paths in the future.

"How about 1789?" the priest suggested.

"Fine," Tim said unenthusiastically. "Do you think we can get in without a reservation?"

"I think so, Tim," Father Hartwell said with an assuring smile.

The VW crossed over the arching bridge spanning the Potomac and inched into the midday Georgetown traffic.

CHAPTER 2

B lade Anthony had lived in the same townhouse on Thirty-Third Street Northwest all her life. Her parents had bought the home in the 1890s before Georgetown was a fashionable address in the nation's capital. Blade's parents were already deceased when, at age thirty-one, she married Joseph Dilorio, a wealthy grocery wholesaler from Baltimore. Her parents died from tuberculosis, the same disease that would ironically claim her husband's life only three years after they married.

After the untimely death of Joseph Dilorio, Blade reverted to her maiden name, Anthony. Having a last name that ended in a vowel other than "e" was, at least in Blade's opinion, something of a social stigma. This was an aversion she had been able to overcome during her husband's lifetime because of his extraordinary good looks. The fact that this first-generation Italian immigrant had also made a fortune in the grocery business was helpful for the three years Blade was forced to circulate in Washington society with a foreign-sounding name.

At the time of her engagement, Blade was living in the family's Thirty-Third Street townhouse with her older unmarried sister, Betina. Since Blade had no intention of moving to Baltimore after she married, a condition she made quite clear to her future husband, Blade lobbied to have her sister move out of the home so that she could continue living in the family residence after her marriage. Betina reluctantly took an apartment on Capitol Hill, which she ostensibly reasoned to her friends was closer and more convenient to the National Archives, where she had worked since graduating from Mount Holyoke. Although the elder of the two girls, Betina had always deferred to her younger, prettier sister. Betina was commonly referred to as "big-boned," not heavy or overweight, but closer in build to the ancestral hardworking women of the "old country." Blade had the fortune of inheriting her father's classic features and charm. Betina never overcame the feeling of rejection at being cajoled out of the family home by her younger, manipulative sister, and even after Joseph's death, when Blade invited her sister to come back to live at Thirty-Third Street, Betina refused, saying she had grown quite fond of the Hill—away from the rigid social scene of Georgetown.

During their brief three-year marriage, when the Joseph Dilorios resided in the classic townhouse on Thirty-Third, the brass "ANTHONY" nameplate had remained in place next to the front door. There was never any question that this was the Anthony home, regardless of the legal last name of the current occupants. Despite his personal feelings, Joseph Dilorio never expressed distaste for living in his wife's family home, surrounded by the heritage and traditions of an old American name. The Anthonys of Thirty-Third Street were direct descendants of Susan Brownell Anthony, the nineteenth-century suffragist, although the links on the family tree were a bit vague, held loosely together by second and third cousins and a few marriages difficult to trace. Nevertheless, Blade participated in Equal Rights Amendment and pro-abortion parades, living the life of a truly liberated twentieth-century woman.

Years later, when the Susan B. Anthony dollar was first minted, Blade designed a custom card containing an uncirculated coin of her ancestor and sent it to three hundred friends on her Christmas list. Even though the project was costly—the price per card including postage was nearly three dollars and thirty cents—Blade could not pass up such an opportunity to latch onto the skirt hems of her famous relative.

Blade was Tim's great-aunt, although the "great" was never attached to her title. She thought it made her sound ancient. Just as the link to Susan B. Anthony was a bit vague, so was the issue of Blade's age. She admitted to sixty, which meant there was probably a swing of ten years or more on the outside, but then, she looked hardly fifty. "Good bones and good upbringing" was Blade's terse dismissal of her fortune, a legacy she would hand on to her handsome nephew, Tim Halladay. Blade wasn't what anyone would describe as a ravishing beauty, although she did command a presence when she entered a crowded room. Her features were sharp and aristocratic, and "well-groomed" was a description that naturally fit her. Blade's public wardrobe was mostly tailored suits and sensible dresses, making her similar in appearance to a petite Greer Garson. Blade openly liked the comparison, having informally assumed the role of Auntie Mame to her nephew after taking Tim to see Garson at the Broadhurst Theatre in the Patrick Dennis play. Miss Garson had recently taken over the starring role from Rosalind Russell, who had abandoned New York to go off and make the film version in Hollywood.

Blade was Tim's mother's aunt, although the relationship between the women was more like that of sisters. Tim became the focal point of Blade's life after the sudden death of her husband. They'd had no children of their own, and since Tim was born, he had always been treated with special attention. His identical twin brother Jeffrey, born only fifteen minutes after Tim, had died in the delivery room. The twins had been premature, and the first ninety days of Tim's life were spent in an incubator at Norwalk Hospital.

Probably with good intentions, Tim's parents didn't tell him that his twin brother had died at birth. But when Tim was five years old, he woke up late one night to hear screams from downstairs. His mother was crying, engaged in a bitter argument with his father. Tim climbed out of bed and crept to the top of the stairs, peeking through the rungs of the banister to the living room below. His mother was slouched in an antique wingback chair as his father passed in and out of sight, defiantly pacing back and forth across the living room floor.

Tim listened intently and soon realized they were talking about a young boy, a person he did not know. His father kept saying something about the booze—that if it weren't for the goddamn booze, Jeffrey would be alive. That it was the booze that had killed his son. Then in a rage, his father stormed out the front door. The squealing tires of the Lincoln pierced the quiet suburban neighborhood as Tim's father sped off into the night. Curled up in the cocoon-like wingback, Tim's mother sobbed quietly and cried out despondently, "Jeffrey … Jeffrey."

Afraid he might be caught, Tim tiptoed back to his room and pulled the covers up over his head, wondering in the dark who Jeffrey was, this Jeffrey who caused so much grief between his parents. Tim could not go to sleep. Instead he stared up at the ceiling until he heard the sound of his dad's Lincoln pull back into the driveway at daybreak.

During breakfast there was a stony silence as his parents went through the motions of getting ready for another day, his father reading the financial pages of the *New York Times*, putting the paper down only to spread apple butter on his toast. Coffee, orange juice, and toast were his breakfast every morning: a meal structured and routine, like everything else in his life.

Whenever his parents wanted some time to themselves, Blade Anthony took Tim into her stately Georgetown home. Tim looked forward to these visits because Aunt Blade was fun to be with and always had interesting surprises planned. She doted on Tim and let him sleep in her big four-poster bed next to her. She slept in silk nightgowns from Paris that Tim could see through when Blade got up in the night to refresh the silver water decanter she kept on the nightstand next to the bed. He could see the soft triangle of hair between her legs, like a delicate lilac bloom. Frequently, Tim would wake up in the night and crawl out of bed, wearing only his Jockey shorts, and curl up on the Oriental rug on which the four-poster sat. There, with his thumb in his mouth, he would cry himself back to sleep, convinced nobody loved him. After getting up to put a blanket over him, Blade would leave the boy there on the floor until he woke up in the morning. Blade sensed it was now time her nephew slept in his own room and in his own bed, a transition she had resisted.

Blade often took Tim to the Smithsonian, and if it had been his decision, this would have happened every weekend. He loved to peer into the glass cases filled with treasures. His favorite exhibit was the coin collection. The complete sets of Indian Head pennies and buffalo nickels fascinated him. His meager collection consisted of only a few samples of each. Blade nurtured Tim's interest in coin collecting, buying him a few dark blue folders with round cutouts for the money, each labeled for the year and minting location: Philadelphia, Denver, San Francisco, or Washington, DC. Blade saved her change, sometimes getting rolls of coins from the bank, and Tim would pore through the money, searching for dates missing from his collection. He eventually became so selective that he began picking out better-condition coins to replace those already in his blue folders.

It wasn't until Tim was thirteen years old that he had the nerve to ask his aunt about Jeffrey. He was inspecting a pile of pennies spread out on the kitchen table. Blade was filling the teakettle with water when Tim asked, "Who was Jeffrey?"

Blade's silence confirmed Tim's suspicion that something was wrong. She turned from the sink and after an awkward pause asked, "Where did you hear about Jeffrey?"

Blade listened as her nephew related the story of the late-night argument he'd overheard when he was a little boy. She let him talk, sitting down opposite him at the kitchen table. Her tea was getting cold, and after careful consideration of the consequences, Blade told Tim about his twin brother Jeffrey who had died at birth. She defended Tim's parents' decision to keep it a secret that he'd been born a twin; there had just never seemed to be a time when they felt comfortable enough discussing it with him.

Tim pushed the pennies around on the kitchen table and without looking up said, "Oh." He was trying to comprehend the news of a twin brother—this Jeffrey. Blade let the subject drop, hoping that she'd done the right thing and also hoping the issue would go away.

The next day, Blade took Tim to the Smithsonian, and as they were leaving the historic building, Tim asked whether Jeffrey was buried somewhere.

"Whatever made you think that?"

"Nothing. I was just wondering."

"We'll talk about it later," Blade said, avoiding the question, "when we get home." The Jeffrey issue did not come up again when they got home. Tim would pursue the mystery of his twin brother on his own; it was clear that Blade had told him all she was willing to divulge.

The next night, Blade took Tim with her to a small dinner party at the home of the MacKenzies, wealthy friends who lived on M Street in a landmark building that had been home to several senators and congressmen over the last two hundred years. In 1924 the house had been the scene of a famous bootlegger heist when the undertaker, George Ward, drove away to Arlington Cemetery in a hearse loaded with cases of bourbon. The home was now furnished with eighteenth-century antiques and numerous pieces of rare porcelain.

Blade knew she could take Tim anywhere, even into adult, sophisticated situations. Her nephew was well mannered and respectful of adults. If mints or candies were accessible on a coffee table, Tim had to be prodded to accept one, and he'd never go back for a second: he was a model child.

Tim's model-child status began to fade, however, when, on the day after the dinner party on M Street, Blade received a distressing call from Mrs. MacKenzie. It seemed that someone had defaced the Japanese wallpaper in the powder room off the main foyer. The hostess was calling because of her concern over what had been scribbled on the bathroom wall: two curved lines like a set of McDonald's arches, each with an oval eye inside, on either side of a drooping nose and two three-fingered hands grasped over a line-wall. Underneath this recreation of an eerie cartoon character from World War II were words scratched in stick letters: "Kilroy Was Here." But the world "Kilroy" had been drawn through and written over with the name "Jeffrey."

Blade drew in a quick breath, holding her chest, as the woman described the nature of the graffiti. Although Mrs. MacKenzie stopped short of accusing Tim of being the culprit, the phone call alone suggested her suspicion. Perhaps Tim had been ignored by the adults at the dinner party and had done it to gain attention. But this was not at all like Tim. Blade was mortified that her charming, well-behaved nephew would even be suspected of such an atrocious act.

"Oh dear ... oh dear," Blade said, barely choking out the words while trying to compose herself. Immediately, she offered, "Of course I will have it repaired."

Mrs. MacKenzie's icy reply—that the wall covering was irreplaceable, purchased at auction at Sotheby's—left Blade even more stunned.

"There is a man," Blade said quickly, "a man that my sister Betina knows at the archives. He does restoration work on damaged prints and paintings—you know, very intricate and rare things. He does a lot of work for the Smithsonian. I'll have Betina ask him to get in touch with me. I know this is a little out of the ordinary, but I think I can convince him to look at the damage and see what can be done."

Blade was floundering, but this seemed to appease her hostess, if only momentarily. Rather than confront Tim about the incident, Blade chose to let it pass, dismissing it as a childish prank: something any thirteen-year-old was capable of doing.

With Betina's help, Blade was able to track down the man who restored paintings, and as a favor to Betina, he reluctantly agreed to look at Mrs. MacKenzie's damaged wall. For $350, he would remove the ballpoint ink markings.

Blade was unaware that her nephew continued to practice his crude artwork, only now Tim was more discreet in selecting targets. He limited his graffiti to public places where he was in the company of other young artists, so it would be more difficult to trace his identity. The bathrooms of the museums, galleries, theatres, and other public buildings throughout Washington offered an almost unlimited outlet for Tim's strange brand of artistry. He expanded his craft to include restaurants, occasionally going beyond the privacy of a restroom to leave a mark on a menu or a matchbook. Tim carried at least two ballpoint pens with him wherever he went, ready to inscribe his eerie logo signature at any opportune time on any virgin surface. What had started as a curiosity became an obsession, and the more signatures of Jeffrey he scribbled on the walls of public bathrooms, menus and the insides of matchbook covers, the more his desire grew to expand onto bigger and bolder canvases.

The turning point came when he went to the men's room of the National Theatre at intermission during one of the many matinees he attended with Blade. There, on the inside of the stall where he was urinating, was the familiar sight of the rounded arches and the beady eye dots above the words "Kilroy Was Here."

Tim immediately drew the same signature on the opposite wall. There, in the last stall in the men's room of the National Theatre were two identical ghostlike faces, gazing across at each other like Narcissus in a mirror. The only difference was that on Tim's image "Kilroy" had been crossed out and replaced with "Jeffrey." The delight he felt at this discovery motivated him to explore bolder opportunities. He diligently practiced his craft for the next two years, careful not to repeat the mistake of being exposed when he'd first scribbled on the Japanese wall covering in the powder room of the M Street mansion. His canvases went public but with safe anonymity. Bus benches were an early breakthrough, followed by the advertising cards inside buses.

In public places Tim was forced to work with different tools. Ballpoint pens had been adequate when he started out, but his work now required the use of Magic Markers and even a small penknife for the harder surfaces like wooden city benches. Tim was selective in choosing his targets, careful not to damage private property.

The ultimate expression of Tim's art came in the form of spray-can paint. This expression had already exploded into subway cars in New York, but the medium quickly became popular in other cities, eventually reaching the nation's capital—first in the city's black and ethnic neighborhoods, then gradually appearing in commercial sections of Georgetown. Tim was fascinated by the ornate beauty of the twisting curls of colored ink spelling strange names and secret codes. He knew this art form would be the ultimate expression of his craft.

As a special treat, Blade got tickets to *Camelot* at the Majestic Theatre in New York. She wanted to see the musical while Julie Andrews and Richard Burton were still in the cast. WhileTim enjoyed the play, especially Roddy McDowall running around in tights, the highlight of that trip to New York was their visit to the Metropolitan Museum. In the gift shop, off the main lobby, Tim picked out several art books and postcards with scenes of the various exhibits and permanent collections. At Blade's urging he also obtained a tote bag to carry all his new books. The words "The Met" were stenciled in large black block letters on the side of the tan canvas bag.

As they were descending the vast stone steps of the museum, approaching the taxi stand on Fifth Avenue for the ride back to the Algonquin Hotel, Tim realized that his problem of how to transport aerosol paint cans and Magic Markers had been solved. No one would suspect that a well-dressed young man, obviously interested in the fine arts and carrying a souvenir of his visit to the museum, would actually be transporting his own subversive materials for a mission most people would hardly view as a cultural contribution to society.

The Met tote bag became something of a signature with Tim, who lugged it around Washington wherever he went. As Tim had anticipated, no one suspected that beneath the books and magazines, drawing pads, and rolls of Life Savers he had stuffed into the tote bag, he was also secretly carrying spray cans and Magic Markers for his obsessive habit. Blade was pleased her nephew had become interested in art, so much so that he made sure to carry sketch pads and notebooks with him in his tote bag. To make the deception even more believable, Tim took up drawing and watercolor painting, and he actually showed signs of becoming a serious artist.

One early afternoon in September, just after Labor Day, as Blade was driving Tim to Union Station for the trip back home to Westport, they stopped at a traffic light at Fourteenth Street. As usual, the top of Blade's red Buick Electra convertible was down. Even in the muggy and humid Washington weather, Blade refused to put the top up. "What's the point of having a convertible?" she would argue. She hated air conditioning and never turned it on.

While they were stopped at the red light, a big city bus pulled up alongside the Buick convertible, belching an offensive cloud of exhaust into the open car. Blade had a running battle with the monstrous city buses that annoyingly cut into traffic lanes, intimidating drivers of smaller vehicles.

Blade glared to her right at the public vehicle as the traffic light turned green. She was about to press hard on the gas pedal to move out ahead of the bus when she saw a chillingly familiar image. On the advertising display card affixed to the side of the bus was a fluorescent blue, spray-painted figure of the double arches with oval eyes. The words "Kilroy Was Here" were printed in childlike stick letters beneath, but the name "Kilroy" had been scratched through, replaced with "Jeffrey."

The bus lunged right, turning onto Fourteenth Street, curving the display card out of view, but Blade was certain it was the same image that had caused her so much embarrassment with Mrs. MacKenzie four years earlier.

The car behind them honked because Blade remained stopped at the intersection, even after the light had changed to green. Blade finally drove forward slowly, as Tim turned around to the car behind them and flipped the driver the finger.

"C'mon, Blade," Tim urged impatiently. "We're gonna be late for the train."

Blade drove silently down K Street wondering whether she had actually seen what she thought, or it was just a fantasy. Even though she had never confronted Tim about the incident at her friend's house on M Street, she felt Tim was responsible. With the image of the two arches and beady eyes burning clearly in her mind as she drove, and the childlike stick lettering beneath, Blade calmly turned to Tim and asked, "Why Jeffrey instead of Kilroy?"

Without a beat, Tim smiled and answered, "Because J comes before K."

CHAPTER 3

"God ... an actual parking place," Tim observed with relief. "I don't believe it." He angled the dented VW into a narrow space between two other cars on the sharply sloped Georgetown side street. Tim locked the car, more out of habit than fear that someone would steal his battered Beetle. He and the Jesuit slowly walked the worn cobblestones in the stately Georgetown residential neighborhood. The sun was shining brightly through skeleton branches of elm and maple trees lining the block. It was oddly warm for the first week of December. Neither Tim nor the priest had bothered to wear a coat.

"It's supposed to snow tonight," Father Hartwell said, breaking the silence, "but it sure doesn't feel like it right now."

"It will seem strange to have Red lying buried in the ground and then covered with snow. Thinking of someone's first night in the ground is strange. It probably gets easier after a while ... you just forget about it. But the first night is ... well, strange." Tim let the thought drift off into the December afternoon air.

As they approached the 1789 the priest said, "If it's busy, we can always wait at the bar."

"After this morning, I'm certainly up for a drink," Tim conceded.

They crossed the commercial block where the restaurant was located next to an antique shop and art gallery. The 1789 was a landmark, a favorite watering hole for the Georgetown faculty and for many members of Congress. The Tombs, the downstairs taproom, was a student hangout. Tim had spent many beer-sodden evenings there on weekends he was up from Williamsburg. Tim was now in his senior year at William and Mary, and throughout his college days he had often made the three-hour drive up to DC to stay at his aunt's townhouse.

Although his initial forays into Georgetown nightlife had started with the Tombs, Tim was soon exploring more interesting and avant-garde locales. Just down the hill on M Street was a small club called the Cellar Door. There was no sign on the corner door; you had to know where it was. The club was owned by the same people who ran Mr. Henry's, the only somewhat openly gay establishment in the city. To order a drink at the Cellar Door, you had to be seated, which discouraged mingling with and meeting other patrons. Even so, it was a relaxed if smoky little club where the decidedly mixed crowd was friendly, and a young singer named Roberta Flack mesmerized audiences with her rendition of "The First Time Ever I Saw Your Face."

One night, while listening to the budding songstress, Tim was approached by a cute guy sitting across the same table drinking beer. "You want to go somewhere a little more interesting?"

"What do you mean?" Tim asked, puzzled but interested.

"I've seen you at the Tombs, and I think I know you from somewhere," the young man said, extending a hand. "Have you ever been to Buenos Aires?" he asked.

"No. Never been," Tim responded.

"I don't know. You look very familiar," the kid said. He was a freshman at Georgetown. They continued to chat over another beer while Roberta continued her set, which was concluded by a standing ovation from the audience.

"Wanna go?" the freshman asked.

"Sure," Tim said, emboldened by the last beer. "Want me to drive? You said this place was in Foggy Bottom."

"Let's cab it. The police are taking down license numbers, and you don't need that."

Tim agreed, and soon the two were out on M Street, hailing a cab. After a short ride, they got out in front of a warehouse in a dark, industrial-looking part of town. Tim noticed a number of black town cars parked along the street, with drivers in dark suits and sunglasses standing by, waiting. It looked oddly like a lineup for a funeral procession.

Tim's new friend paid the doorman who was screening patrons waiting to get into this mysterious venue, and then they were inside a cavernous warehouse. The place was blaring with disco music and flashing strobe lights. The boys picked their way through the pulsating crowd to a long bar at the far side of the room, where the freshman from Georgetown ordered two beers with coupons the doorman had given him.

"Different, huh?" he said, raising his drink to their surroundings as they looked out on the scene. A boy clad only in a Speedo was dancing atop the bar, prancing gingerly between drinks, as patrons threw dollar bills at his feet. Tim soon caught on to the routine. For ten dollars, the boy would let you touch him. For twenty, he would lower the small bathing trunks to reveal a full hard-on. And for fifty dollars, he would let you suck his cock.

The hostess at 1789 greeted them warmly. "Hello, Father Hartwell. I didn't know you were coming in today."

"We should have called," the priest said, starting to apologize, but he was cut off by the friendly woman.

"Nonsense," she chided cheerfully. "You know I can always find a place for my favorite servant of the Lord. Two for lunch?"

"Yes, just the two of us."

"Give me a few minutes. A couple of tables are on coffee; we'll give them a prod. Have a drink at the bar, and I'll be with you in no time."

The gracious greeting Father Hartwell received from the hostess at 1789 was not unusual. He was a well-known, popular figure throughout Washington, on a first-name basis with the maître d's and bartenders at the city's finest restaurants. He played golf regularly at the Congressional Country Club and was a frequent guest at luncheon and dinner parties at some of Georgetown's most recognized addresses. He was a fixture at Blade Anthony's townhouse on Thirty-Third Street, always one of the first names on her guest list whenever she was planning to entertain.

Some of the Jesuit's colleagues were quietly critical of the flamboyant lifestyle Father Hartwell exhibited, seemingly more appropriate for a wealthy playboy than for a priest who'd taken a vow of poverty. The Father Rector of the university held a different opinion. He saw the value of Father Hartwell's popularity with the wealthy and influential: the priest was a good ambassador for the university, merely socializing and not acquiring personal gain for himself, at least not in any tangible, materialistic way. In many respects he was carrying on the traditional Jesuit role in the courts of kings and emperors. Father Rector needed an emissary to fulfill his fundraising goals, and no one on his staff was more perfectly cast or more qualified to perform that task than Father Hartwell.

In addition to his social popularity, John Hartwell, as he was known in the secular world, had by the age of thirty-five published six volumes of literary criticism and a collection of short stories and had several of his poems accepted in various magazines, including *The New Yorker*. He chose to teach freshman English at Georgetown and to conduct an advanced creative writing workshop for graduate students. His reputation among the faculty, at least scholastically, was one of esteem.

"What's your pleasure?" the priest asked Tim.

"Just a beer," Tim answered.

"Sure you couldn't use something stronger?"

"No, that's okay. Beer is fine."

"Heineken here for my friend, and I'll have a Dewar's on the rocks," the Jesuit instructed the bartender. "This is on me today," he insisted. "Payment for the ride back."

"Thanks," Tim said, a little self-conscious that a priest was buying him a drink.

"To better days," the priest toasted.

"Yeah," Tim sighed, taking a long swallow of the cold beer.

The 1789 was crowded, as usual on a Friday afternoon, with the overflow spilling into the bar. They had been lucky to get two seats since people were now pushing behind them, trying to get the attention of the bartender, who was extremely agitated. He was cursing about the bar not being properly set up from the night before: no lemons or mixers and no clean glasses. It was obviously not a good day for him.

The commotion in the crowded bar made conversation difficult, if not impossible. The few minutes promised by the hostess turned into half an hour, time enough for Tim and the priest to finish a second round of drinks before being called to their table in the dining room.

"Sorry, Father," the hostess said apologetically. "You would have thought these folks had checked in for the entire weekend."

"No problem, Margaret," the priest reassured the woman, whose name he of course knew. "We're not in a hurry."

The hostess picked up the bar check and in a commanding voice called to the harried bartender. "I need a round on the house for these two patient gentlemen. Send them to window three," she ordered, as the bartender glared disapprovingly.

"This is excellent," Father Hartwell said as the hostess sat them at a large table adjacent to the windows overlooking the Potomac. "Well worth the wait."

"Thank you, Father," she said, blushing. "You're always so kind."

The complimentary drinks arrived along with the lunch menu on a chalkboard. By this time Tim's anxiety had ebbed, and the events of the morning seemed far away. Tim and the priest looked out upon the brilliant December afternoon. A long, flat barge was cutting through the sparkling surface of the river, approaching the arches of Key Bridge, separating the two men from their illustrious friend whose coffin was being sealed into a cement casing and covered over with earth. The two sat quietly sipping their drinks, each immersed in his own private thoughts of Red.

"She was the youngest WAC ever to receive a regular army commission," Father Hartwell mused as he finished his scotch.

"Yes, and she was the youngest officer commissioned since Custer. She told me that once, and I always thought the two of them had a lot in common—Custer wearing his flamboyant red ties in battle and Red with her hair and defiant personality."

The Jesuit smiled at Tim's comparison of the notorious young Civil War general and the actress.

"So why no fanfare at Arlington?" Tim questioned.

"I suspect there was some discomfort at the Pentagon with reconciling Janet Matthews of *Another World* with the WAC poster girl. Also, Allan is still in Norwalk Hospital. There may be some issues, as he was driving. So the decision was made to keep it very low-key, except of course for the Mass at St. Patrick's yesterday."

Red's husband, Allan, had been driving their small Triumph TR4 on the New England thruway after the cast wrap party for *Another World* when he apparently fell asleep at the wheel and slammed into a bridge overpass near Norwalk, Connecticut. The small sports car was ripped in half, leaving Allan in a coma with massive internal injuries. His radiant wife had been decapitated.

"What will you do with the flag?" Tim asked.

"I'll make arrangements to get it to Allan as soon as he's out of the hospital. The university will make sure it is taken care of properly."

The waiter came to the table to recite the daily specials. Both men listened politely and then ordered cheeseburgers, medium rare, with fries.

"That was simple," the waiter smirked, unimpressed with their selections, as he removed the chalkboard menu.

"Have you changed your mind about applying to grad school at Georgetown?"

"What, has Blade on her crusade with you again?" Tim asked, irritated by the all-too-familiar topic.

"No, of course not," the priest answered. "But we both know how your aunt feels about your turning down the undergraduate scholarship."

After Assumption School in Westport and then four years of regimented Jesuit training at Fairfield Prep, Tim had been eager for a change. The strict and inflexible teachings of the Catholic Church were at odds with the young man Tim was becoming.

To appease the Jesuits, Tim had applied to Georgetown while at the same time submitting applications to Harvard and to William and Mary. Tim was rejected by Harvard, accepted at William and Mary, and offered a scholarship to Georgetown. For Tim, the decision was obvious: William and Mary, even though it created tension at home and with his aunt Blade, who would have preferred having her handsome nephew around the corner from her townhouse on Thirty-Third Street.

"I thought we'd ended this discussion a long time ago," Tim said dryly. "Besides, it's all academic because I'll never get a deferment."

"You could at least apply," the priest commented. "A wise man always allows time to reconsider."

"Cut the Thomas Aquinas stuff," Tim laughed.

"All right," the priest smiled, backing off. "You're sounding like Red."

After first meeting Red as Cleopatra at the Olney Theatre, Tim had accepted her invitation and had enrolled in her acting class that fall in Westport. From the time they met, Red was drawn to Tim. He was handsome, shy, and sensitive, qualities she had imagined her own son would have possessed had he lived.

Red taught a small class for young people at the White Barn Theatre, where she worked with the legendary actress Eva LaGallienne, with whom she shared billing in a production of *Ghosts*. It was there that Red directed Tim as George Gibbs in *Our Town*. They'd rehearsed the famous soda fountain scene for hours until Red was pleased with the timing of the pantomime. It was the hardest acting challenge Tim had ever undertaken. He remembered Red's direction as relentless and demanding.

Red had sent Tim a telegram from Kuala Lumpur on opening night of the William and Mary production of *Our Town*. She told Tim she was sorry she couldn't be there, but playing Cleopatra in Malaysia was proving a challenge that would keep her out of the country until the soap opera began shooting again. She told Tim not to forget everything they'd worked on with George and Emily at the White Barn workshop last year. Tim proudly taped the exotic telegram from the soap opera star onto the mirror in the cast dressing room backstage at Phi Beta Kappa Hall. It was the last time he heard from her.

"I know how close you were to Red," Father Hartwell said quietly. The two stared at their half-eaten cheeseburgers, saying nothing. Tim regretted ever having introduced the priest to his actress friend. Red had been in DC for a Veteran's Day program honoring wounded Vietnam servicemen, and Tim had invited her to a cocktail party at his aunt's home. Blade was delighted to have the famous TV actress on her guest list, but both she and Tim were annoyed when Father Hartwell monopolized Red in conversation for most of the party and then invited the actress to dinner.

"Will you be at your aunt's brunch on Sunday?" the priest asked, trying to change the mood.

"She's having a brunch?" Tim asked.

"Didn't she tell you?"

"I don't know. She might have. The last few days have been really fucked up."

"Well, I'm sure Blade will expect you to be there," the priest commented matter-of-factly.

"Who's coming?"

"I suppose the usual suspects. Your aunt said she was expecting twelve people. A small group."

Blade always managed to assemble an interesting mix of guests, careful to include new faces. She made a point of inviting a few younger people when Tim was going to be there. Truthfully, Blade was more drawn to the younger guests than to her longtime friends and regulars. Red had been one of Blade's favorite guests because she had added a dimension of glamour to any party. But although Blade had welcomed the actress to her home whenever she was in town, there had been a distinct competitiveness between the two women when it came to Tim.

"I think she thought it might cheer you up," the priest said.

"Probably," Tim agreed.

"I know …" the priest commented inconclusively. He then gestured to the waiter, who approached the table. "Coffee here, please. Tim, coffee?" the priest asked.

"Yes, sure." Pushing away from the table, he announced, "I've got to hit the men's room first. Those Heinekens are starting to travel."

The priest nodded as Tim made his way through the crowded dining room to the restrooms on the other side of the bar. Without thinking, the Jesuit put twice as much cream as usual in his coffee, pondering whether he should breach the subject of JoEllen with Tim or just let him find out on Sunday.

JoEllen Taylor was a pretty graduate student at Catholic University. Tim had first met her at Olney when she escorted him backstage to see Red with his bouquet of narcissus. She was an apprentice at the time, with a small role in the Shakespearean play. She was friendly and a bit taken with the starstruck young kid. Two years older than Tim and very confident, she abruptly asked Tim out when she saw him leaving Red's dressing room. Tim was so taken by JoEllen's aggressiveness that he immediately accepted. No girl had ever asked him out before. That was the start of a relationship that would continue the next two years whenever Tim spent time in Georgetown.

Father Hartwell sat at the table idly stirring his cream-filled coffee, wondering whether he should tell Tim that his aunt had invited JoEllen to brunch Sunday. When Blade had called, she'd asked the priest his opinion about including JoEllen. The young girl had accompanied Tim to his aunt's social gatherings many times, and even though she was an attractive and smart young woman, Father Hartwell suspected Blade was not particularly fond of her.

"She's a charming, bright young lady," Father Hartwell had responded diplomatically.

"I've always thought so," Blade had acknowledged, choosing to take the Jesuit's comment as approval. Her motivation was quite simple: she thought JoEllen, a friend of the late actress, might help her nephew cope with Red's death.

Father Hartwell was signaling the waiter for the check when Tim rejoined him at the table. The priest had decided to mention JoEllen, rather than risk Tim suspecting later that he was in collusion in some way with Blade.

"I believe your aunt has asked JoEllen for Sunday," the priest said offhandedly.

"What?" Tim said.

"She asked me what I thought when she called the other day," the priest explained.

"That's classic," Tim said, laughing. "Really classic," surprising the priest who was expecting quite a different reaction.

"You mean you're not upset?"

"Shit, no. JoEllen and I are still friends, even though we're not dating anymore."

Father Hartwell wondered whether the cavalier attitude was for his benefit or whether Tim really didn't care.

"It's just funny ..." Tim smiled. "I never thought my aunt liked JoEllen. That's all."

The Jesuit inspected the check and placed a twenty-dollar bill facedown on top of it. The waiter returned, and Father Hartwell said, "That's all right. We don't have to wait for change."

"Thanks for lunch."

"Payback for the ride," the priest said again.

"Anytime."

The dining room had almost emptied out by the time the two left. The air outside had become distinctly cooler, and faint layers of cirrus clouds rippled across the afternoon sky as a jetliner arched its way gracefully up into the impending cloud formation, having just taken off from National Airport.

"Looks like we're going to get that snow after all."

"Guess so," Tim agreed, conscious that they had slipped back into the banality of talking about the weather. "You need a lift anywhere?" Tim offered, knowing the Jesuit would decline.

"Thanks. It's a short walk, and after three drinks I could use the fresh air."

"Okay ... I guess I'll see you on Sunday," Tim said as the two stopped at the corner.

"I think your aunt said eleven o'clock."

"That means we won't eat until one," Tim laughed.

"See you then," the priest said as the two turned in opposite directions.

Tim was a few steps into the crosswalk when the priest turned and called out, "Tim!"

He stopped and turned back to face the priest, who was only a short distance away on the sidewalk.

"You know Red had a really full, beautiful life. We should remember that and remember all the joy she brought to those who knew her. We should remember the happiness of her life and not the sadness of her death."

Tim studied the priest for a few seconds without responding. Pulling his blazer collar up against the chilly afternoon air, Tim replied curtly, "See you Sunday."

CHAPTER 4

JoEllen Taylor was born in Elkton, Maryland, the second of five children of John and Marybeth Taylor. Being the only daughter in the family, JoEllen enjoyed a number of privileges not accorded to her four brothers. She was the only child to receive new clothes, and even after her older brother David grew an inch taller than his father, his "dress clothes" were more likely to come from his father's closet than from the J. J. Newberry department store on Main Street.

It was not easy being an independent plumber in Elkton, Maryland, raising a pack of five children, but John Taylor was a proud man, a hard worker who prided himself on not drinking or smoking. God help his kids if he ever caught one of them indulging. It was only after Ned, the youngest boy, was born that John gave in and allowed his wife to go to work. Marybeth took a job as a sales clerk at Newberry's. The extra money helped out, as did the 15 percent employee discount on all merchandise she purchased. After a while, Marybeth's take-home pay diminished to barely a few dollars a week, once deductions had been made for time payments on merchandise she'd bought, mostly for JoEllen.

Marybeth was a petite woman, almost frail, and when her daughter rejected a skirt or blouse she'd brought home from a clearance sale, clothes that in JoEllen's words were "creepy" or "old-fashioned," Marybeth would end up wearing them herself, too embarrassed to return the items to the store. JoEllen wanted only the latest fashion designs advertised in the Sunday supplement.

Although JoEllen was the princess of the family, the boys were not overlooked. There was money for new basketball sneakers, guitar lessons, or whatever the current fad. But it looked to her brothers like JoEllen didn't have to lobby quite so hard to get whatever she wanted. It was the general consensus in the family that JoEllen was talented, gifted: she had a pretty singing voice and a naturally coordinated sense of rhythm that made her one of the fastest learners in her ballet and tap dance classes.

JoEllen took classes at Arianna Foote's School of Dance in Elkton. Arianna had been a Rockette at Radio City Music Hall for eight years before returning to her hometown to open her own dance school. Her credentials as one of the leggy precision dancers on the big stage in New York City made Arianna something of a celebrity in Elkton. She taught classes to the town's young ladies in a small loft above the dry cleaners on Normira Avenue. The rest of her plans for settling down in Elkton hadn't materialized.

Arianna had dated her classmate Bobby Devlin through high school before going off to New York for her career in show business. Bobby had enlisted in the navy while Arianna was doing five shows a day at Radio City, but it wasn't until after Bobby was discharged from the service and came back to Elkton to run his father's Shell Oil station that they ran into one another again. Arianna stopped at the filling station to get gas; she was back in Elkton for the short break before the Christmas pageant opened.

Bobby began going up to New York whenever he could get away from the gas station, to see Arianna dance in precision with all the other Rockettes. He had a hard time picking her out since to him they all looked exactly alike. Arianna let Bobby stay in the apartment she shared on West End Avenue with two other Rockettes. For the first year, Bobby slept on a rollaway bed in the small living room while the three Rockettes shared the one bedroom. Eventually, the sleeping arrangements changed, with Arianna's roommates taking the rollaway while Bobby and Arianna slept together in the bedroom.

Bobby continued his courtship of the young starlet, overwhelmed by the glamorous crowd that Arianna ran around with in New York— glamorous to Bobby anyway; he thought being recognized by a waitress at the Carnegie Deli was a sign of fame and success. But to Arianna, having to wait at Sardi's for a table along with everyone else not currently in a Broadway show was a sure sign of failure.

For all the time that Arianna had been working as a Rockette, she had been hoping to get a part in the chorus of a big Broadway musical. Then she might move into a featured role or understudy, anything to get her out of doing five shows a day as a Rockette.

But despite the many auditions she went to, the result always ended up the same: she was either too tall or too thin (which meant small breasts). When Bobby was first allowed into her bedroom, he was exposed to a private world of Arianna's he had not known. After they made love, Bobby drifted off into a contented sleep with Arianna nestled snugly in his arms, but then he woke up to Arianna sobbing quietly as she lay beside him.

"What is it?" Bobby asked concerned, fearing he'd done something to hurt her.

"Oh, it's stupid," Arianna said bitterly, breaking out of Bobby's embrace and sitting up.

"What?" Bobby asked, confused and still worried that he was somehow at fault.

"Don't you see ..." Arianna said, frustrated her boyfriend didn't understand. "Don't you see that I'm never gonna do anything more than kickin' and tappin' five times a day? Five times a day every goddamn day." Arianna broke into sobs as Bobby moved up and pulled her into his arms, stroking the back of her head.

Bobby began going to New York more often, hoping he might be able to lure Arianna away from the city and the world of show business that was making her so unhappy. But Arianna forged on as a Rockette and continued to audition for Broadway shows and road companies. She even tried out for the Jones Beach summer theatre, but was again turned down. The painful reality of her lack of options was gnawing at her, making her bitter and vulnerable. So when Bobby proposed on Christmas Eve, after she had performed the nativity pageant and had seen the gothic organ rise out of the orchestra pit one more time, Arianna accepted, leaving her job at Radio City Music Hall and returning to her hometown to marry Bobby Devlin.

Arianna moved back into her parents' modest wood-frame house, across from the same elementary school she'd attended. She soon realized that her assessment of a failed stage career was not how her family or the people of Elkton perceived her—not at all. To them, she was a celebrity, a famous person who even signed autographs.

Arianna's father had been with the town's fire department all his working life, and he arranged to have a banner strung across Main Street from the firehouse that read, "Welcome Home, Arianna." When she first saw it as she stepped off the Greyhound bus that brought her home, she thought it was corny. But when she realized the sentiment was genuine, she began to think that maybe she was being too hard on herself. After all, there were only forty-eight Rockettes at any given time, girls from all over the country, from all over the world, many of whom had dreamed of being up on the big stage, admired by the scores of people who visited Radio City every year, and then marching in Macy's Thanksgiving Day parade, where they were seen by millions of people, on network television.

One day while she was exercising at the YWCA gymnasium, stretching and doing simple combinations, a young girl Arianna didn't know came up and asked, "Miss Foote … would you show me how to do that?"

A bit taken aback by the young girl's openness, but at the same time flattered that she knew her name, Arianna said, "Well, sure, honey. I'd be happy to show you. It's not really that hard."

At first, Arianna put notices on the bulletin board at the YWCA, reserving the gymnasium at seven-thirty Saturday mornings, the only time she could access the gym before other scheduled activities. She was terrified the first week when five teenage girls showed up. Arianna began with some basic exercises and positions. To her surprise, the girls caught on quickly, and the second week, when ten girls showed up for the early Saturday morning class, the Arianna Foote Academy of Dance in Elkton, Maryland, was officially born.

Embracing her new career and her celebrity status, Arianna withdrew a thousand dollars, more than half her savings, and took a lease on a second-floor loft space above the Courtesy Dry Cleaners on Normira Avenue. She had the floors sanded and varnished to a high gloss; she installed walls of mirrors and a wooden barre rail around three sides of the room. The Arianna Foote Academy of Dance was the first such cultural establishment to join the Elkton Chamber of Commerce, which was dominated by marriage chapels and motels. Elkton was famous as the wedding capital of the US Eastern Shore because the city required no waiting period, no blood tests, not even witnesses. Droves of young couples, as well as celebrities such as actor Cornel Wilde and singer Billie Holiday, descended on Elkton for quickie weddings.

Bobby Devlin was not enthusiastic about his prospective bride's career as a dance teacher. He openly objected to her spending money out of her savings account to open the studio, money he felt could be applied, along with his own, toward a down payment for a house. Arianna brushed Bobby's objections aside, pointing out that the studio was an investment. They wouldn't be able to make ends meet on what Bobby took away from the Shell station, so she was going to have to work.

Thus began the rift between the two lovers. Bobby had taken over the Shell station when his father died the previous year, and he was proud to have his own business. He was hurt that Arianna considered his income inadequate. Bobby thought his fiancée had given up her show business career when she'd accepted his proposal and moved back to Elkton. Now she was running a dance studio, talking about giving recitals, and even forming a local dance company to train young people for professional careers. It was as though Arianna was trying to live out her own dreams vicariously through her students.

As she performed her daily exercises and taught her class of young women, Arianna studied herself in the mirror. She gazed at her other self in the reflection, seeing the maddening career that had eluded her in New York. In her dance studio Arianna was the star, the focus of attention.

The problem now was her relationship with Bobby Devlin. A growing tension festered between them, a tension that came to the surface at the Frank 'n Stein, a local restaurant and Bobby's favorite. Their one-night-out-a-week Saturday date was dinner at the Frank 'n Stein. Arianna dreaded going to this local greasy spoon with its corny name. But Bobby, being practical and wanting to save money for their marriage and the house they would someday buy, resisted Arianna's coaxing to go somewhere else.

"This place gets worse all the time," Arianna fussed as she looked around the neon-lit dining room while pushing the overdone chopped steak around on her plate.

"Isn't this place ritzy enough for you?" Bobby snapped.

"It's not that. I'm just sick of coming here," Arianna said. "Every Saturday, all we do is come to this stupid place."

"You used to like coming here," Bobby fired back. "You too good for the Frank 'n Stein all of a sudden?"

"Well, it might be nice, just once in a while, to go somewhere different. Just once in a while go into Wilmington, or someplace at the shore. Somewhere nice for a change instead of this dumb place every Saturday night."

"Sure ... and spend a lot of money for nothing. Just to go to a fancy restaurant."

"Oh, you don't understand," Arianna said in disgust. "You don't understand anything."

"What I do understand," Bobby said, "is that you've got highfalutin pipe dreams in your head about a lot of things. Like all of a sudden you're too good for everything. Like you're some sort of queen floating around with your dancing classes and everything … like you're better than everybody else."

Bobby hadn't meant to lash out at Arianna, but she'd made him feel inferior with her jibes about the gas station and the Frank 'n Stein. Bobby was beginning to wonder why Arianna had come back to her hometown and why she had accepted his proposal in the first place. Since she'd returned to Elkton, it seemed nothing met with her approval, and nothing mattered to her except her dance studio.

The rift between Arianna and Bobby grew, and the breaking point came when Bobby surprised her one Saturday night, picking his fiancée up and driving her to the outskirts of Wilmington to the Wagon Wheel restaurant. Bobby had asked one of the drivers who delivered fuel to his Shell station if he knew any good places to eat up near Wilmington. The guy had recommended a place called the Wagon Wheel, and it had sounded perfect to Bobby.

Ironically, the Wagon Wheel turned out to be a mirror image of the Frank 'n Stein, which made Bobby immediately comfortable. It was one of those places that had opened as a diner and expanded when they'd gotten a liquor license—adding on a large dining room with red plastic booths. The music on the jukebox was mostly country and western, and each booth had its individual accordion selection box, into which Bobby immediately pumped four quarters.

Arianna tolerated the place until their food arrived. When her crab cake dinner was placed in front of her with french fries instead of the coleslaw she'd ordered, she threw a fit. She pushed the plate aside and refused to eat. Bobby tried to get the waitress's attention to correct the order, but Arianna just fumed and pouted, insisting that they leave. She couldn't decide whether Bobby was playing some kind of sick joke on her or was just an insensitive redneck.

Bobby wolfed down his chicken-fried steak and left money on the table as Arianna stormed out of the restaurant to wait in the parking lot. During the drive back to Elkton, the two didn't speak, but Bobby could see Arianna was biting her lip to hold back tears. He couldn't believe someone could get so upset over french fries.

Bobby pulled up in front of the Foote family house and stopped the car. Arianna looked for a moment like she was on the verge of releasing her anger, but instead she abruptly bolted out of the car, slamming the door behind her and retreating into her parents' house. Bobby shifted the car into gear and angrily peeled away from the curb, confused and upset over his fiancée's peculiar behavior. He drove back to his apartment and drank a full six-pack of beer, staring into the television set while trying to understand what he'd done so wrong to upset Arianna.

The next day, Bobby found a note in his mailbox from Arianna saying she was sorry for the previous night. She was sorry for a lot of things, but since she had moved back to Elkton, everything had changed. She said it was just no use; she could not get married, not right now anyway, and she was breaking off their engagement. She was kind, though, saying it was probably all her fault, and Bobby was a good person who deserved someone he could be happy with. She was very sorry, she repeated.

Bobby crumpled the letter in his fist and immediately drove to the Footes' home to confront his fiancée. Arianna's father opened the front door, expecting Bobby's visit, and said that his daughter would not see him, that she was resting in her room. Mr. Foote looked as confused and baffled as Bobby.

A few days later, Arianna moved out of her parents' house and into a small apartment near her dance studio. She expanded her classes, now teaching older women who were more interested in shedding a few pounds than in the art of dance. Arianna needed the money, so she set up separate classes for her more mature students. There were only so many young women in Elkton serious about ballet lessons.

Arianna was faced with a different challenge when Johnnie Izzo came into her studio one afternoon; he wanted to take dance lessons at her academy. Johnnie was considered a freak by most Elkton townspeople. He was a delicate, pretty Italian boy who had worn makeup and tight clamdigger pants to class when he attended Elkton High. He was bullied and ridiculed by his more macho classmates. He once came home with a black eye and two broken ribs, his clothes torn and soiled by urine. He had been raped by some of the basketball players in the gym locker room when he was caught peeking at the boys taking showers after practice. Johnnie told his parents he'd fallen off his bicycle trying to outrace a coming freight train at the Main Street/Mayberry crossing. But everyone knew you didn't get broken ribs and soiled clothes falling off a bike.

Johnnie dropped out of Elkton High after that incident and went to work in his family's restaurant, the Arrow, the only authentic Italian pizza and spaghetti place in Elkton. Johnnie worked in the kitchen doing prep and washing dishes, out of sight of customers in the dining room.

On Friday nights, when the kitchen at the Arrow closed at ten, Johnnie rode his motorcycle to Wilmington, where he performed at a weekly drag show at the Sands bar. He donned a blond wig, put on makeup, lipstick, and eyelashes, and then slipped into a slinky white negligee to make his entrance on the makeshift stage through silver tinsel streamers. Johnnie's drag name was Mariland Monroe, and once in the pink spotlight, he looked very much like his idol. He sang breathy renditions of "My Heart Belongs to Daddy" and "Little Girl Blue," and the crowd of beefy, beer-drinking guy bears and bike lesbians loved their beautiful, soft Mariland. After his set, Johnnie would pick up the dollar bills hurled onto the stage. Then he'd change into his jeans and ride his motorcycle back to Elkton, returning to the Arrow for another week of cleaning the grease trap and stuffing dirty pizza cartons and empty cans of tomato paste into the dumpster in the parking lot behind his family's restaurant.

Arianna agreed to take Johnnie on as a student, charging him two dollars per private lesson on Friday mornings. They worked on basic positions and movements. Each week, Johnnie became more like the real Marilyn, and Arianna began to feel a special affection for the beautiful young Italian drag queen.

Gradually, Arianna spent more and more time in her studio. When she wasn't teaching, Arianna did exercises in front of the three mirrored walls. She began to choreograph elaborate, lengthy dance pieces for herself, dances that had no chance of ever being performed for an audience because of their length and complexity. It was as though Arianna were composing the pieces for the person in the mirror, as though she were teaching the dances to her other self.

Arianna began to wear black leotards with only a long shirt or small jacket whenever she went out on errands or to the bank. When he ran into his daughter on the street in her dance attire, Arianna's father grew red with embarrassment. He pretended not to notice when the other firemen at the station cracked jokes about the sensual lady in black tights.

Arianna became another freak, like Johnnie Izzo, in the town where she'd grown up. She'd moved back to marry her high school boyfriend in Elkton, the town where it was so easy for celebrities and young couples to get married overnight with no questions asked, where it was so easy for anyone to get married—except, ironically, for Arianna.

CHAPTER 5

"It looks like it's getting ready to snow," Blade called to Tim as he entered the front parlor where she was sitting in the crewelwork wingback chair doing the *New York Times Magazine* crossword puzzle. She was curious to see her nephew, whom she hadn't spoken to since breakfast the day before. Tim had left right after finishing his coffee Thursday to take the train to New York to attend the funeral Mass at St. Patrick's. He'd stayed in the city until evening, waiting to take the milk train back to Washington. It was after two when he got back to Georgetown, and Blade had long since gone to bed.

Tim had spent Friday morning working in the greenhouse and had not come up to join his aunt for breakfast as usual. He hadn't felt like talking to anyone before leaving for the cemetery.

"The radio said there could be three to five inches of snow," Tim reported as he approached his aunt and kissed her lightly on the cheek.

She looked up at him and murmured, "Probably won't stick, though. The ground is still warm."

Tim picked up the *Washington Post* folded on the coffee table in front of the fireplace and sat on the sofa opposite Blade. The two were walking through a scene as though nothing out of the ordinary had happened in the last forty-eight hours.

"You're probably right," Tim agreed. "What did the paper say?"

"I don't know," Blade said. "I didn't get much of a look at it this morning. Besides, they never get it right."

Tim flipped through the paper, turning to the obituary section to see whether Red's funeral was reported. A terse statement appeared, more like a legal notice, saying that Sara Ryder was interred at Arlington Cemetery in a private ceremony. That was it. Nothing else.

"A cold period in Spain?" Blade asked.

"Huh?" Tim responded suddenly, drawn out of his thoughts.

"A cold period in Spain," Blade repeated. "I need a five-letter word for a cold period in Spain."

"Oh, that," Tim said. "You and those stupid crossword puzzles."

"I know," Blade sighed. "I get so frustrated, especially with the *Times Magazine*. I don't know why I even bother. I used to think I had a good vocabulary, but these things make me feel so inadequate."

"I don't know why you let yourself get so worked up about some dumb crossword puzzle with words that nobody has ever heard of, or even uses," Tim chided.

"I suppose you're right. But it is kind of fun when you get on to one and everything just falls into place."

Tim smiled. "You'll never change," he said, returning to his newspaper.

"At least I still do them in pencil," Blade offered. "Not like Mrs. MacKenzie at the club, who sits there every Sunday after brunch and fills in the boxes of the *New York Times Magazine* puzzle using a ballpoint pen. The gall ... to sit there in front of everyone and fill in the words without a mistake. I'm surprised the Congressional Club tolerates such behavior. The worst part is she doesn't read books. Maybe newspapers and magazines, but nothing you'd call literary. I just don't understand it."

Tim had heard this repartee before, usually when Blade was stumped on a word. She would bring up Mrs. MacKenzie, whom Tim remembered as the lady from M Street whose Japanese wallpaper had been mysteriously defaced during a dinner party several years ago. Since that evening, Blade and Mrs. MacKenzie had not socialized, choosing to drop each other from the list of guests invited to their many brunches and cocktail parties.

"Spain ..." Blade mused. "I don't know what they mean by 'a cold period.' I'll skip it for now. Maybe the other letters will fill it in."

As Blade went back to her crossword puzzle, Tim flipped through the pages of the paper. A few minutes passed until Blade was stumped on another annoying clue and got fidgety.

"And another thing," Blade continued. "That MacKenzie woman does jigsaw puzzles upside down. She turns all the pieces facedown and works on the puzzle from the shapes alone. Never even looks at the colors or the design of the picture. She turns over the pieces on the card table in the club library and proceeds to do the puzzle by herself ... facedown. None of us who might like to find a piece to fit in and maybe participate has a chance."

Tim did not respond to his aunt's commentary on Mrs. MacKenzie, choosing instead to focus on the newspaper.

"You got in late last night," Blade said quietly. Tim was free to come and go as he pleased whenever he stayed at his aunt's townhouse. He didn't have to report his activity; he was a young adult.

"It was after two o'clock," Tim said vaguely. "As usual, the train was late—just stopped dead for over an hour outside Baltimore."

"Oh," Blade said, waiting for more, but when Tim went back to the newspaper, Blade chimed in to keep the conversation going. "I thought they had improved the train service. You hear all those ads about how it's actually quicker to take the train to New York than the air shuttle. I mean, by the time you get into a cab to the airport and go through the same thing once you get to LaGuardia, you could have been there on the train ... and it's a lot less expensive." Blade rambled on like a recording, starting to irritate Tim.

"You shouldn't believe everything you read in advertisements," Tim said curtly. "Most of it's a lot of bull." He picked up the sports section and effectively cut off the conversation. Blade fretted in the big wingback chair, frustrated that she was unable to penetrate her nephew's mood and talk to him.

"I'm having a few people tomorrow for brunch," Blade said brightly, persistent in her efforts to get Tim to open up. "I hope you can stay before driving back to Williamsburg."

"I know," Tim answered flatly. "I saw Father Hartwell."

"Oh," Blade said curiously. "He's coming, of course."

"I had lunch with him," Tim said, anticipating his aunt's question. And with that Tim stood up, folded the newspaper neatly, and placed it on the coffee table. "I've got work to do in the greenhouse before dinner." Tim knew if he stayed longer, his aunt would want to discuss the funeral, and Tim didn't want to talk about it.

Tim was nearly out the doorway of the parlor when Blade called, "Tim, if you have time can you try to trim those dead limbs on the dogwood tree? It should be done before winter sets in. That tree is so pretty in the spring, and I want to make sure that nothing happens to it."

"Sure. I'll take care of it," Tim assured his aunt, and he was off down the stairs to the garden apartment below.

Blade tried to concentrate on the crossword puzzle, but her mind kept wandering. Tim's reticence troubled her. The phone rang, bringing her out of her concerned reflection. It was Barbara, Tim's mother, calling from Westport. She was on the verge of hysteria.

"It's everywhere!" Barbara shouted into the phone.

"Now calm down," Blade said soothingly.

"I know ... I know ... but it's like a horror movie," she continued, trying to control herself. "I never know when this weird thing is going to hit me in the face. It sends a chill right through me. Oh, Blade, it's gotten so I'm afraid to open a drawer or even a book."

Tim's mother had made the startling discovery when she was having the living room of the Westport house repainted. The pictures had been taken down from the walls, and books from the shelves on either side of the fireplace had been removed. Barbara first noticed curious scribbling on the brown paper backing on one of the pictures stacked against the dining room wall. At first she thought it might be an imprint by the artist or the framer, but when she examined it more closely, she realized it was something quite different. The double arches encasing the eerie oval eyes hovered over the childlike, stenciled words "Kilroy Was Here," with "Kilroy" crossed out and over it "Jeffrey" stenciled in. The recognition of the name sent a shock through Tim's mom.

She quickly put down the picture and thumbed through the others stacked in a pile against the wall. To her horror, each had similar markings, some with two or three images in various corners on the back panel. The scribbling had been done with felt-tip pens and Magic Markers.

Barbara went to the empty living room, drawn by some intuition that there was more to this secret, as though she had uncovered a hidden code. She examined the bare walls, the faded paint having left discernible squares and rectangles where pictures and paintings had hung in place for several years since the room was last painted. Tracing the defined spaces lightly with her fingertips, she flinched as she came across the same curious markings on the painted wall, only this time drawn lightly in pencil. Some of the surfaces had more figures than others, but all were in corners. Then, as final confirmation that there was some meaning to this series of images, she selected a painting from the stack in the dining room, one that had three markings in the corners. She held it against the outline on the wall where it had hung. The three images on the back of the painting were mirrored in pencil, back-to-back, on matching places on the wall.

Driven by curiosity, Barbara then went to the emptied bookcases by the fireplace to discover yet more examples of the eerie graffiti on the shelves. The books stacked in boxes in the dining room were her next target. She became frantic as she opened each volume to find the same mocking eyes peering from within the arches over the words "Jeffrey Was Here." Practically every book, except the most recent arrivals from the Book-of-the-Month Club, had been defaced.

Barbara immediately went to the liquor cabinet and withdrew a bottle of vodka to pour a generous drink into a water tumbler. The burning sensation on her tongue and the warm rush down her throat calmed her as she sat dazed at the kitchen table. Barbara was not one of those Westport wives who drank in the afternoon while waiting for her husband to come home from the station: she was not a John Cheever character study. She thought of herself as a good woman, one who went to Mass every Sunday, a woman who had raised two children and who did volunteer work at Norwalk Hospital. She'd sat at the kitchen table for a long time, pouring a second glass of vodka, before picking up the phone to call Blade.

"It's just a young boy's prank," Blade reasoned unconvincingly. "You're attributing too much importance to this nonsense." Blade thought for a moment and then spoke carefully. "There may be something at the root of all this, but I'm sure it's not serious." Then before her niece could respond, Blade added, "Let me think about it a bit and call you back. Will you be home later this afternoon?"

"Yes, I'll be here."

"All right. I'll talk to you later. And for god's sake, don't get so upset. I'm sure it's quite harmless."

Blade thought for a few minutes after putting the receiver down and then quickly picked it up again to call her confidant, Father Hartwell. Blade was not a particularly religious person, other than going to Mass regularly on Sunday. She'd long dismissed the holy days of obligation and confession as old-fashioned, along with "meatless Fridays," but Blade did rely on advice from her friend, Father Hartwell. She was relieved when she reached him at his Georgetown office that afternoon.

"Hello, John," Blade said cheerfully. "I'm so glad I caught you in." Blade and Father Hartwell had long been on a first-name basis. After attending so many social functions together, they'd dispensed with the priestly formality. "There is something I need to talk to you about if you have a few minutes."

"Of course. Anything for you."

"It's about Tim," Blade started, not knowing how to go on.

"Yes?" the priest said.

"You see, John, he's been going through this period."

"What kind of period?"

"I know this is going to sound silly, but Tim has been writing graffiti for some time now. He's defaced walls and paintings and books in his parents' home—and I believe even bus posters around the city. There are probably other places that I'm not aware of. At first I thought it was a childish prank he would outgrow, but I'm afraid it's still going on." Blade was picking at her nails nervously as she shared this information with the priest. She felt as though she were in confession.

"What graffiti?" Father Hartwell asked. "What does it look like?"

"Do you remember that logo 'Kilroy Was Here' that was such a pop culture icon after World War II?"

"Sure, of course. It was everywhere for a while."

"Well that's the graphic but with an identical matching image on a wall, or on a facing book page, as though it were reflected in a mirror."

"Very creative," the priest said appreciatively.

"It's not funny," Blade snapped, irritated.

"No, of course not. I'm sorry. I didn't mean to imply that it was." The priest was familiar with similar situations, dating back to Germany in the Middle Ages. He thought about the *doppelganger* theory, the belief that everyone in the world has a double. There were various interpretations and manifestations, ideas that a person's double could appear as an image, a ghost, even as a twin.

"There's more," Blade went on. Father Hartwell was silent. "The word 'Kilroy' is scratched out of this graffiti and the name 'Jeffrey' penciled in above. On every image."

The priest instantly made the connection of Jeffrey, Tim's twin brother who'd died at birth. That put an eerie, fascinating twist on the *doppelganger* theory.

"I see," Father Hartwell said. "When did this behavior start?"

"About six years ago when Tim was almost twelve. There was an incident at a friend's house on M Street. Tim accompanied me to a dinner party, and he was the only young person there. It was probably a mistake to bring him, but he was always so well behaved and polite around adults, and I didn't want to leave him alone while I was out having a good time."

"Didn't he always go with you to social functions?"

"Yes, I took him everywhere. He was a precocious child, and my friends adored him. You know. You've known Tim since he was a little boy."

"So this incident at your friend's house on M Street …?"

"The Kilroy graffiti showed up on the antique wallpaper in her powder room. Mrs. MacKenzie didn't accuse Tim, but it was obvious she believed he was responsible. I mean, is that something another guests would have done … no matter how much they'd had to drink?"

"Unlikely," the priest agreed. "Did you ever confront Tim?"

"No! I didn't know what to say," Blade confessed.

"Do you want me to talk to him?" Father Hartwell offered.

"I'm not sure. I know you two have issues."

"Yes, but I think they're unfounded."

"It has something to do with Red, doesn't it?"

"Yes," the priest said without explanation.

"Then maybe it's not a good time for you two to have a discussion about this graffiti business."

"You're probably right. As always," Father Hartwell said warmly. "Anything else I can do for you?"

"I'll be fine," Blade assured him. "I just wanted to share this with someone I trust. But I'm worried about Barbara."

"You can call me anytime."

"Just show up Sunday and be your charming and witty self."

"Would not miss one of your lovely brunches," the priest said, trying to end the conversation on a bright note.

"Oh, John, by the way, do you know a word for a cold period in Spain?"

"What?" Hartwell replied, caught off guard.

"I need a five-letter word for a cold period in Spain."

CHAPTER 6

JoEllen Taylor, who would go on to become Arianna's star pupil, had to lobby long and hard before her parents gave in and allowed her to start taking dance lessons. Although they were supportive of their daughter's creative ambition, money was already going out for weekly piano and voice lessons, and now JoEllen wanted to go to a dance studio. The Taylors were a bit skeptical of Arianna and thought the lady who paraded around town in black tights was eccentric.

But as with everything else she wanted, JoEllen was successful in breaking down her parents' objections, and she began going to the beginner's ballet class at Miss Foote's every Saturday morning at age twelve, making her the oldest pupil in the class. She concentrated hard on the lessons, never taking her eyes off Arianna, ignoring contact with other girls in the class. At home, she would practice positions for hours before the full-length mirror on her closet door.

Arianna noticed that her new student was catching on quickly, but JoEllen's frustration whenever she missed a step or failed to pick up a combination the first time caused Arianna concern, so she asked JoEllen to stay after class one Saturday. Arianna praised her new pupil for her remarkable progress, saying that she had learned in several weeks what it took most of the other girls months to get down. Arianna asked JoEllen what drove her so hard and what had caused her sudden obsession with dance. Arianna knew that it wasn't just a fad for the girl; JoEllen's determination was deeper than that of any ordinary impressionable twelve-year-old.

JoEllen confided that she was going to be a star, and part of her training and preparation required that she learn how to move, especially how to dance. She worked hard because she'd started later than most of the other girls and felt she had to catch up. Arianna was impressed by the young girl's resolve and that she had planned out her future. For the first time, Arianna saw hope that one of her students might go on to a successful career in the professional world of show business.

JoEllen continued her classes, arriving early and accepting Arianna's invitation for extra private lessons at no charge. But JoEllen wanted more. She begged her parents to let her take additional classes. She wanted to study jazz and modern dance as well as basic ballet. JoEllen's parents were frustrated, confronted with the reality of the lack of money for all their daughter's lessons and classes: it was simply more than they could afford. JoEllen understood that she came from a working-class family and, as a concession, decided to drop her piano and voice lessons. She could read music proficiently, and she had a natural talent for singing, although not quite the perfect pitch that her parents boasted. The discipline of dance classes, now three times weekly, challenged JoEllen, and in two years she'd perfected her technique far beyond all the other students.

Because of the popularity of her dance academy, and because many of her students were young girls who attended Elkton High, Arianna was asked if she would help the drama teacher stage the yearly spring play. Traditionally, the event had been predictable high school play material: agonizing Shakespearean comedies and amateurish musical revues with a theme.

Charles Alberton, the new drama teacher and a graduate of Carnegie Tech, had far greater expectations for his rural Maryland students, and he immediately recognized a valuable asset in Arianna Foote. After all, she had performed professionally on the great stage at Radio City.

The spring program would be Alberton's first production for Elkton High since joining the staff. His true love was musical comedy, and he was determined to make his first offering a spectacle unlike anything Elkton had ever seen.

As an undergraduate at Carnegie, Alberton and his roommate and lover, Richard Ekstrom, had written and produced an original musical based on the life of Lola Montez. The production was well received, even if the material was deemed a bit obscure. Lola Montez was Irish by birth, but in the mid-nineteenth century she became famous as a Spanish dancer and then as the mistress of King Ludwig I of Bavaria. The highlight of the Alberton/Ekstrom show was the staging of Lola's famous "Spider Dance," where she lifts her skirt so high that the audience can see that she is wearing no undergarments. When she then becomes enmeshed in a web, she does a frenzied, exotic dance, finally freeing herself and disappearing up into the theatre flies sixty feet above the stage. Encouraged by favorable reviews, Alberton was convinced he and his lover would go on to become the next Rodgers and Hammerstein. That hope was dashed when right after graduation Richard announced he was marrying his high school girlfriend, whom he had dated off and on as an undergraduate, seemingly as a cover for his affair with his roommate. Shortly afterward, Charles Alberton accepted the position as head of the drama department at Elkton High.

Early in the school year, Arianna and Alberton began discussing material for the spring production: it was a foregone conclusion that it would be a musical, which was fine with Arianna, provided it have a plum role for JoEllen. They settled on *Oklahoma*, for its historical importance in the world of musical theatre and because with minor editing—no kissing or swearing onstage—it could be mounted pretty much intact.

Arianna handpicked JoEllen to dance the lead in the famous dream sequence, a ballet that Arianna choreographed to showcase her star pupil's talent. Although the consensus was that the production was the most professional Elkton High School had ever put on overall, everyone singled out JoEllen as the star performer.

That was the spring of JoEllen's sophomore year. All that following summer and throughout the fall, she continued to study dance at Arianna's academy, hopefully preparing for another featured role in the next high school production.

Arianna and Alberton debated long over the selection of the spring musical; both had motives affecting the final decision. Although *Oklahoma* had been well received by the faculty and parents, there had been some rumblings about doing a more contemporary show, something the students could readily identify with. It was that thinking that led to the selection of *Bye Bye Birdie* as the spring production. Arianna objected, arguing that the show had little cultural merit, but she admitted it would probably be very popular. Arianna's real objection, although not voiced, was that the choreographic opportunities were limited, requiring little more experience than the students got from gyrating on the school gym floor during homecoming and prom nights. The main factor in Arianna's reticence was that there was no appropriate showcase role for JoEllen.

Reluctantly Arianna conceded, and as expected, the show was a huge success, which required the scheduling of an extra weekend of performances. JoEllen sang and danced in the chorus, more or less unnoticed, while a pretty young freshman with a birdlike voice was cast in the female lead. Certainly no one could accuse Arianna of playing favorites by giving all the good parts to students in her dance class.

Arianna used cunning the following year when the same debate arose over the selection of the spring musical. Alberton was lobbying for *The Fantasticks* even though the musical required a relatively small cast and had no complicated dance numbers. Arianna knew JoEllen would graduate from Elkton High that year, and she was determined to showcase her star pupil's talents that she had nurtured over the past four years.

The final decision for the Elkton High spring production was *Carousel*. True, the musical posed huge challenges for Alberton and Arianna: they would have to edit the script extensively because of the dark nature of the material, but the music was beautiful, and there were many opportunities for flashy dance numbers. The production also required a large cast, thus opening opportunities for many students.

JoEllen was cast as Julie Jordan, the female lead, and even though her singing voice didn't send chills through the audience, her extraordinary dancing did. Arianna choreographed two solos especially for JoEllen. So when it was announced at graduation that JoEllen had won a full scholarship to study dance and theatre arts at Catholic University, not one person was surprised. Arianna glowed at the thought of her star pupil going off to seek the career that had so frustratingly eluded Arianna herself.

JoEllen's luck continued when she was selected as an apprentice at Olney Theatre that summer before her freshman year at Catholic University. And when Mrs. Taylor ran into Arianna at the bank one day and said her daughter had a small part in *Antony and Cleopatra* along with professional actors from New York, Arianna decided to take the bus to Olney to surprise JoEllen.

Arianna was waiting backstage when a pleasant, shy young man carrying a bouquet of white flowers asked her for directions.

"Oh, I'm just waiting to see one of my students, one of the apprentices," Arianna replied apologetically. "I'm not … no, I'm not in the company."

"I see," Tim said politely.

The two unlikely visitors hovered by the stage entrance as the cast and crew went about their assigned duties, setting up for the evening performance. A bearded young man in a sweaty T-shirt and denim overalls asked if he could help them, and Arianna inquired about whether JoEllen Taylor was backstage.

"Sure, I'll send her over," the friendly young man answered, disappearing behind the network of ropes and dangling canvas backdrops that would magically create the Egyptian empire during the play. A few minutes later, JoEllen appeared carrying a wig stand—a faceless wooden skull covered by a long, silky black wig, which JoEllen was brushing—as she looked around to see who was waiting for her. A broad smile beamed across her face when she spotted Arianna by the stage entrance. She rushed to embrace her teacher, still clutching the wig stand, creating an odd illusion of two figures with three heads.

"Arianna ... what a surprise!" JoEllen gushed. "Why didn't you tell me you were coming?"

"I wasn't sure until the last minute," she said vaguely.

"And who's this?" JoEllen asked, eyeing Tim.

"Oh, we're not together," Tim quickly explained. "I'm Tim Halladay. I'm here to see Miss Ryder ... I mean, if she'll see me."

JoEllen escorted Tim to Red's dressing room, and then she and Arianna moved to the Green Room, where a simple buffet of cold cuts, potato salad, pickles, and soft drinks had been set up for the cast, crew, and their guests. Arianna was thrilled to be part of the gathering; she immersed herself in the surroundings and fantasized she was back in the theatre world, and not just a visiting dance teacher from a rural Maryland town. She and JoEllen talked happily about Elkton and the school plays and about the courses JoEllen would be taking at Catholic University in the fall.

"I hope you're continuing to work on your jazz and modern dance programs," Arianna said, sounding almost motherly.

"I'll take a class once or twice a week when school starts, but mostly just to stay in shape and keep my movement fluid. But I've decided I'm never going to make it as a dancer. I want to concentrate on my acting and voice lessons," JoEllen announced casually, unaware of the stinging pain her words brought to Arianna.

"But all your work ..." Arianna stuttered, as though something were being ripped out of her.

"Red tells me I should make up my mind what I want to do and then go after it single-mindedly," JoEllen went on. "I've decided I really want to act. God, if I could have a career like hers—I mean, to play Cleopatra someday! My life would be fulfilled," JoEllen said dreamily. She had no idea of the crushing rejection she'd brought down on Arianna.

"And another thing," JoEllen continued, innocently oblivious. "Red says that most dancers couldn't act their way out of a burning building." This further sent a sword through Arianna's newly battered heart.

The stage manager announced that it was two hours to curtain for the evening performance, a polite signal to end socializing and get back to the serious business of theatre.

"I have to get back to work," JoEllen apologized. "Can you stay for tonight's performance?"

"No, dear, thank you. I have to get back."

"Well, it was great seeing you," JoEllen said, gently kissing Arianna on the cheek. "I'll be sure to come by next time I get home."

"That would be nice. I know how busy you are," Arianna said sadly.

Arianna walked like a zombie, slowly and methodically, out to the main highway to wait for the Greyhound bus, which finally arrived after more than an hour. Cars were streaming into the entrance of the Olney Theatre parking lot for the evening performance as Arianna boarded the bus for the trip back to Elkton.

She sat in the front seat across the aisle from the driver, gazing at the highway ahead, where white lines rhythmically disappeared beneath the lumbering, elephantine bus.

"Miss, this is Elkton!" the bus driver said, leaning around to Arianna. "Isn't this your stop?" She looked at the burly driver, as though he were intruding on her private world, and without a word she stood and got off the bus.

"Ya see all kinds," the driver mused as he pulled shut the accordion door and moved the big bus back onto the highway.

It was only a few blocks to Arianna's apartment, and Elkton was quiet on the warm summer evening. Arianna stopped at the liquor store next to the dry cleaners where her studio was located and purchased a pint of whiskey. She didn't bother to look at the brand. She just picked a brown bottle off the shelf. Arianna drank only occasionally, maybe a little wine at dinner, and she had never purchased hard liquor before. She placed the small paper bag in her purse and walked the remaining few blocks to her apartment. At the kitchen table she poured the whiskey, a little at a time, into a coffee cup and drank the acrid-tasting liquor slowly and deliberately, while tears silently rolled down her face.

On Sunday morning when the elderly lady who lived across the hall from Arianna opened her apartment door to let her tabby cat out for his morning run, the smell of choking fumes filled the hallway. The old woman called the police, who had to place handkerchiefs over their mouths as they broke down the door to Arianna's apartment. Windows were quickly shattered to allow in fresh air. Arianna's lifeless body lay gracefully sprawled upon the kitchen floor with her head deep in the gas oven. An ambulance was called, but there was no need to put on the siren and flashing red lights.

Arianna's funeral later that week at the Baptist church was well attended. The Elkton fire department came out in full force, and six firemen in uniform served as pallbearers, out of respect for Arianna's father, who sat dazed in the front pew of the church. Many of Arianna's former students from the dance academy were there as well as their parents; many had always thought that the lady in black tights was eccentric, but they came anyway to pay their respects to Elkton's only Rockette. Elkton was the kind of rural Maryland town where people put differences aside in times of tragedy. The Taylors, JoEllen's parents, and Bobby Devlin were sitting in the pew behind Arianna's father. JoEllen was noticeably absent, unable or unwilling to leave her apprentice duties at Olney to attend her former teacher's funeral. No one commented or made crude jokes about Johnnie Izzo, who sat in the rear of the church dressed in full drag as Mariland Monroe, softly weeping.

CHAPTER 7

Tim got up early on Saturday to work in the greenhouse and to cut the dead branches off Blade's dogwood tree. He wanted to plant narcissus bulbs in the clay pots he had prepared with pebbles so that Blade would have the fragrant white flowers to place around the Georgetown house during the coming dreary months of January and February. Tim enjoyed "forcing" bulbs to bloom within a period of eight weeks, even though he knew they would never bear flowers again after that traumatic process. For Tim it was a confirmation that there was no eternity, no afterlife for beautiful flowers, a belief he held for himself and one contrary to his Catholic upbringing. Blade had ordered a container of five hundred bulbs from White Flower Farm in Litchfield, Connecticut. Tim had divided the bulbs into bundles of twelve, placing them in brown paper bags, and then storing them in the basement apartment refrigerator until they were ready to plant.

Tim patted moist soil over the bulbs and placed six pots, each containing twelve bulbs, in a cool, shaded area of the greenhouse.

He would instruct Duane, whose grandmother was Blade's cook and housekeeper, to move the pots into a sunny area once the bulbs had sprouted. Blade would have a continuing cascade of white flowering narcissus while winter snows dusted the cobblestones outside on Thirty-Third Street.

Next, Tim tackled the dead dogwood branch in the garden. It was not as difficult a job as his aunt had suggested. Tim clipped the few dead limbs dripping with moisture from last night's snowfall, which had been only enough to cover the shrubs and boxwood hedges with a light dusting. Tim broke up the dead branches and stashed them into the green waste container reserved for yard trimmings. Duane would put the garbage bins out on the street Monday for collection.

His gardening duties finished, Tim washed his hands and put on a clean sweatshirt before going up to the drawing room, where Blade was reading the morning newspaper.

"Did you have breakfast?" Blade asked cheerfully.

"I had juice. I'm fine. I just wanted to get some work done early."

"I see you've been busy," Blade observed, looking out the parlor window at the trimmed dogwood tree. "Thank you, Tim. I wanted to get that taken care of before we had an ugly ice storm that might take out the whole tree. That would have been a shame."

"It should be fine," Tim assured her.

"Will you be having lunch?"

"I'll just make a sandwich or something. I've got a lot of studying to do. I need to read two more O'Neill plays before I can start my paper. It's past due."

"Of course," Blade said, a bit disappointed.

"I'll study this afternoon, but I'll be up for drinks and dinner later, about six."

"Yes, that will ne nice." Blade was relieved that she would have her nephew's company that evening.

"I'll be ready for a drink after all that O'Neill." Then he kissed his aunt lightly on the cheek. "See you later." With that he headed down the stairs to the basement apartment.

Tim had cut classes to attend Red's funeral. He now had a lot of work to catch up on, but he had told his professors beforehand, and they all had agreed to work with him. It was well known at William and Mary that Tim was a protégé of Red Ryder, the flamboyant TV star of *Another World*. Tim's mother had heard about the actress's sudden, tragic death on the local Westport radio station while preparing breakfast and had immediately called Tim. The news had spread quickly across campus. Two jocks from Sigma Nu had found Tim on the floor in the hallway of his dorm, sobbing in a fetal position, the receiver of the pay phone dangling above his head. They had carried him back to his room like a dog hit by a speeding car, placing him carefully on his bed and spreading a blanket over his limp, trembling body. They had immediately called the Dean of Men's office.

Now as Tim got a Coke from the small refrigerator in the wet bar, preparing for a long afternoon with Eugene O'Neill, he smiled upon noticing the certificate of merit Blade had framed and hung over the bar. It was Tim's "Counselor of the Year" award from Camp Robin Hood, displayed as proudly as though it were a diploma from Harvard.

The summer before Tim was to enter William and Mary, he'd taken a job as a counselor at an exclusive boys' camp in New Hampshire. His parents had been adamant that he get some kind of paying job to help defray college expenses. His plans for a second summer as an apprentice at the Westport Country Playhouse didn't qualify. When Tim had explained his predicament to Red, she said she had an idea that might work out.

"I have a friend from Yale who runs a summer camp for rich Jewish kids in New Hampshire, and they have some kind of drama program in addition to all the sports," Red explained.

Tim laughed. "Me in summer camp?"

"It might be more fun than caddying at Longshore Country Club," Red pointed out. "Anyway, when I talked to my friend Drew last week, he told me that he had staff lined up for all the sports activities, but he was having trouble finding an assistant for the drama program. He asked if I knew anyone who might be interested. At the time I didn't think of you. I assumed you'd be at Westport all summer."

"Well, that's not going to happen," Tim said.

"Let me give Drew a call and see if he's still looking," Red offered. "You'd be perfect. And it might be fun. I understand the camp is very nice. It's right on Lake Ossipee."

"I guess it couldn't hurt to talk to him."

"His name is Drew Rabinowitz. A really nice guy. His family has run this place for years. Oh, and"—Red paused, trying to suppress a laugh—"it's called Camp Robin Hood."

"God save me," Tim moaned. "Couldn't it at least have some exotic Indian name?"

Tim did get a call from Drew Rabinowitz, who explained that they were looking for an assistant drama coach, someone who could help with the talent show and the annual play put on for Parents' Day at the end of the summer. An opera teacher from Ohio had been hired to direct, but Drew felt he needed an assistant to actually get the shows put on. Tim's work as an apprentice at the Westport Country Playhouse the summer before was exactly the hands-on kind of experience Drew was looking for. The job paid three hundred dollars for the summer, plus all room-and-board expenses. Tim thanked Drew for the opportunity, waited a day, and then called back to accept the job. A week later, he was on a train to Boston, where he transferred to a charter bus that took him over to Center Ossipee, New Hampshire, and to Camp Robin Hood.

Red's assessment that the camp was "very nice" was an understatement. Camp Robin Hood was nestled in the foothills of the White Mountains of New Hampshire. The property sprawled over four hundred acres, with a mile of shoreline on Broad Bay, at Lake Ossipee. Before it was turned into a boys' camp thirty-five years earlier, the property had been the private lodge of one of Boston's most notorious bootlegging dynasties.

The yellow school bus could barely squeeze through the two stone pillars that marked the camp entrance off the main road. The bus lurched down a dirt road, cutting through thick brush and pine tree branches that scraped the side of the bus as it crept into camp. It came to a stop in a clearing next to a huge wooden barnlike building: the main lodge and central hub of Camp Robin Hood. A man came out onto the veranda, bounding down the wooden steps of the porch.

"You must be Tim," he said as Tim stepped off the bus into the dusty clearing.

"Tim Halladay," Tim said, looking around.

The man shook his hand. "Welcome to Camp Robin Hood. I'm Drew Rabinowitz. We spoke on the phone."

"Yes, of course." Tim was relieved to put a face to a name.

"Sorry you were the only one on the bus. All the other guys got in yesterday, but since you were a late addition, we had to make special arrangements."

"Thanks," Tim said, unsure whether special treatment was a good thing.

"Bobby," Drew said, pointing to the driver, "will take your trunk and duffel bag to the bunk. You can unpack and get settled later. First I want to introduce you to Andy."

"Andy?"

"My father. The founder of Camp Robin Hood. Although he's supposed to be retired, he's still the king around here," Drew said proudly. "He's anxious to meet you."

"Okay," Tim said nervously, not sure he was ready for an audience with the king.

Drew and Tim walked up the steps of the veranda where the senior Mr. Rabinowitz was standing, arms folded and smoking a pipe.

"Dad, this is Tim Halladay, our new assistant drama coach."

Andy Rabinowitz was a burly, bearlike man, perhaps in his seventies; it was hard to tell because he was in such excellent physical condition and sporting a full, gray, bushy beard. He reminded Tim a bit of the actor Gabby Hayes. Like all the other staff members, as Tim would soon see, Andy wore the official Robin Hood uniform: dark green knee-length shorts and a white T-shirt emblazoned with the camp logo.

The king greeted Tim warmly by putting a hairy arm around his shoulder. "You're going to be a welcome addition to our merry little family, Timmy. Now Drew will show you around and help you get settled. See you at supper."

Tim followed Drew along a dirt path toward the lake where ten wooden cabins were spaced along the waterfront. Tim was assigned to cabin number two, named "Robin's Roost," his new home for the summer. Just inside the screen door, Tim saw two full-size bunks, each with a small chest of drawers and a nightstand with a reading light. These were the sleeping quarters for the two counselors assigned to Robin's Roost. Completing the arrangement were two rows of neatly made cots, six in all, each with its own small footlocker. At the rear of the cabin were two sinks and two enclosed toilets. The cabins had been designed with the comfort and privacy of the campers and counselors in mind—not exactly roughing it in the woods. Daily maid service was provided for cleaning the cabins; laundry was deposited in canvas bags and placed on the beds for Friday pickup. Everything was returned Sunday cleaned and neatly folded. The only housekeeping chore required of campers was that they make their bed before assembling for roll call.

"Tim, meet Mike Ross, group leader for Robin's Roost." Drew introduced Tim to a clean-cut young man who was folding socks and placing them on the bottom rack of the nightstand at the edge of his bed.

"Pleasure," Mike said, extending a hand to Tim. As group leader, Mike was in charge of the cabin and technically Tim's supervisor. "I understand this is your first time at Robin Hood."

"Yes," Tim said, trying to sound confident. "I'm really looking forward to the summer."

"It can be a great experience," Mike offered. "As long as you don't let the kids get to you."

"I'll let you two get settled," Drew said, excusing himself. "See you at supper." He closed the screen door, leaving the two counselors to themselves.

"This is my third year here," Mike continued. "I think I've got the system down pretty well. The first year was kind of rough, but then I caught on."

"What do you mean?"

Mike looked at Tim squarely. "You see, the kids that come here are ... well ... different. I mean they're not like you and me."

"I understand they're mostly from pretty wealthy families, some even kids of celebrities."

"You'll see soon enough," Mike laughed. "Don't get me wrong. They're mostly good kids. Just different. You'll see."

Tim finished unpacking his duffel bag, which had been placed on his bunk by Bobby the bus driver, and arranged his clothes into neat stacks inside the small dresser next to his bed. Mike excused himself and went down by the lakeshore to have a cigarette. About an hour later, a loud clanging on a metal triangle announced supper. Tonight it would just be staff and counselors because there was still one more day of orientation before the campers arrived. Tim had missed meetings earlier in the day because of his late arrival, so Drew took him around before sitting down to dinner, and introduced him to the staff and other counselors, about fifty people in all, whose names Tim immediately forgot. That wouldn't be a problem, however, since everyone knew Tim or knew about him: he was the hot topic of conversation as the youngest counselor ever hired at Camp Robin Hood. The minimum age for counselors was usually twenty, and Tim would only turn eighteen in a few weeks, well after camp started. Drew had made an exception, after a long discussion with Andy, for two reasons: (1) he was desperate to find someone to help with the drama program, and (2) Red had assured Drew that Tim was a very responsible young man and mature well beyond his years.

The drama program was in disarray this season. Drew had learned late in April that Woody Perkins, one of his father's cronies who had run the program for over twenty years, would not be returning. His chronic emphysema had progressed to the point where Woody's doctor absolutely forbade him to attend camp again this summer. This had come as a blow to Drew, who had always let Woody run the drama program with no supervision or interference, especially since both the talent show and the final play were hugely popular events.

Drew had quickly placed ads in several college newspapers with reputable drama departments and received some impressive résumés. After interviewing four candidates and being turned down by three, Drew had offered the position to Anthony Esposito, a college professor at Oberlin who taught opera at the institution's prestigious Conservatory of Music. Although, as he had noted in his report to his dad, Drew thought Anthony was a bit eccentric, his credentials were impeccable. Anthony's eccentricity had surfaced a week before his arrival at Camp Robin Hood, when he sent Drew a telegram saying that his assistant, David Cohen, would accompany him to the camp for the summer. Annoyed, but in an untenable situation, Drew had given in and created a staff support position for David.

"This is Anthony," Drew said nervously as he introduced Tim to the new head of the camp drama program. Anthony was standing next to the massive stone fireplace in the dining room, smoking a cigarette, and talking to two other staff members. Unlike everyone else, who was dressed in the green and white camp uniform, Anthony wore a long flowing caftan that only partially concealed his girth. His long, curly black hair and full beard projected a Jesus-like image as he held court in the dining room. David Cohen stood silently a few steps behind him, nervously cracking his knuckles.

"It's a pleasure," Tim said, extending a friendly hand.

"All mine," Anthony said, taking Tim's hand as he looked closely at his handsome new assistant. "I hear you apprenticed at Westport."

"Yes, I was there last summer." Tim was pleased that Anthony knew something of his background.

"That should come in handy. I know quite a few people at the Guild," Anthony said, seemingly trying to impress Tim. "Excellent group." He was referring to the American Theatre Guild, the legendary institution that ran the Westport Country Playhouse.

"Oh, and this is David. He's here to keep *Mother* out of trouble."

"Hi," Tim said, slightly taken aback by Anthony's flamboyance.

"He'll be providing the musical backup for all our productions this summer," Anthony explained.

"Great. I look forward to working with both of you," Tim said.

Drew had retreated to the other side of the great hall to join his father and other staff members, leaving Tim time to get better acquainted with Anthony and David.

The bugle pierced the crisp New Hampshire air, announcing reveille as it did at seven o'clock every morning except Sunday, when the campers and staff were allowed to sleep in. Today was the last day of orientation before the campers would arrive, and Tim had a lot to learn. One thing was immediately apparent: camp life was regimented. Posted on the bulletin board outside the screen door of Robin's Roost was a schedule of the day's activities, which Tim studied intently:

WEDNESDAY, JUNE 27

7:00 a.m.	Reveille
7:30	Breakfast
8:00	1. Work assignments
	2. Group leader meeting
12:00 p.m.	Lunch
1:00	Group leaders' meeting with staff
3:00	Specialists (as announced, meet at office)
4:40	Closing discussions and questions
	(Social Hall—all staff)
5:45	Buffet (Andy's cottage)
8:30	Movie (*Me and the Colonel*—Danny Kaye)
	Social Hall—optional

The next morning after breakfast, the group leaders did a final inspection of their assigned cabins, making sure all was in order for the imminent arrival of the campers. On his bunk Tim found a list of the six boys who were assigned to him and for whom he would have primary responsibility. A brief bio of each young man and his family background was included. It read like a page out of *Who's Who*. Two of the boys were sons of US congressmen, one's father was a senator, another was the grandson of the chairman of CBS, and the other two were the products of Wall Street and Madison Avenue tycoons.

"I told you." Mike winked and gave Tim a good-natured jab in the ribs as he was studying the roster. "Different from you and me."

"Are they all like this?" Tim asked, amazed.

"Pretty much, although you seem to have lucked out with some of our more famous guests. But all these kids are from rich families; otherwise, they couldn't afford to come here for eight weeks. Christ, my tuition at MIT for a whole year is less than what it costs to send a kid to Robin Hood, just to learn how to shoot a bow and arrow."

The group leaders and their assistants were lined up at the twenty-nine cabins spread out around the lake and nestled in the pine groves and meadows circling the Social Hall. Campers were divided into groups based on age, not by athletic ability or any skill. The youngest campers, the Tinker-Pagers, were eight years old or would turn eight during that calendar year. Tim was assigned to the next group, the Jugglers, who were nine. Although these boys would be Tim's primary responsibility for day-to-day activities, his job as assistant drama director would bring him in contact with campers of all ages. Boys were accepted at Camp Robin Hood up to fourteen years old. This summer, there would be a total of 157 campers. Supporting them were eight staff members, thirty-six counselors, and twenty-seven paid workers for administration, maintenance, and commissary duties. The staff-to-camper ratio at Camp Robin Hood was higher than most luxury resorts in the Catskills or Miami.

Just before noon, the caravan of ten chartered yellow school buses, escorted by three staff Jeeps, turned off the main paved highway and onto the rutted dirt road for the last mile of the journey to Camp Robin Hood. Drew and a few of the senior staff members had gone into Boston early that morning to meet the boys at South Street Station and at Logan Airport to make sure each camper was accounted for and onto the right bus. Each bus displayed a large, neatly lettered placard in the window designating a camper category: Tinker-Pager, Juggler, Squire, Archer, Yeoman, Lancer, and Friar. Like everything at Camp Robin Hood, the arrival of the campers was extremely well organized and supervised, with nothing left to chance.

Drew hopped out of the lead Jeep, clipboard in hand, and started directing the bus drivers to pull up and park in a line behind the main flagpole that towered in front of the Social Hall. Between shrill blasts on the whistle he wore around his neck, Drew barked orders to the drivers as they discharged their precious passengers to waiting staff members. The boys were each given a cool, wet washcloth to freshen up and were then led into the main dining room in the Social Hall. There, twenty-four tables, set for eight diners each, were neatly arranged in three rows before the huge stone fireplace. Signs posted on the tables indicated where the campers were to sit, according to their designated rank. On a raised platform at the far end of the hall were three more tables, where Andy, Drew, and the other senior staff members were to dine, overlooking their charges. The administrative, maintenance, and commissary personnel ate in a separate room off the kitchen, at long picnic tables.

As the campers were being ushered in to their assigned tables, Andy rose on the platform, microphone in hand, to give his traditional welcoming speech. The boys who had been there previous years rolled their eyes and smirked at the familiar banalities about camaraderie, sportsmanship, and the band of "merry men, gentlemen" that made up the family of Camp Robin Hood that now filled the great hall. Andy received a cheering round of applause when he concluded his remarks. He then signaled to David Cohen who was sitting at the upright piano on the platform. David cracked his knuckles and immediately struck the opening notes of the national anthem, pounding on the slightly out-of-tune piano as the boys and the staff sang the familiar words. With "the home of the brave" still reverberating throughout the great hall, the mood was broken only by the thundering racket of hundreds of chairs being dragged across the wooden floorboards as the boys took their seats for lunch. An army of young men and women neatly dressed in khaki shorts and white polo shirts immediately descended on the room, placing a cup of hot soup in front of each newly arrived guest. All meals at Camp Robin Hood were served by local teenagers hired from Center Ossipee and North Conway. They worked three meals every day, with only Sunday evenings off, when the staff hosted a weekly campfire dinner for the boys. The waiters were paid minimum wage, but they received their meals, if not the exact food served to the campers. It was a good eight-week gig in rural New Hampshire, where summer jobs were otherwise scarce. The waiters also shared in the season-end bonus of gratuities, which was substantial, provided by grateful parents. This money was distributed at the owner's discretion among counselors and staff. Direct tipping to individual employees was discouraged, but that policy was not enforced.

Soup was followed by a choice of chicken, beef, or fish, a hot meal at every lunch. If campers were finicky eaters, and there were several every year who were, the kitchen would go out of its way to accommodate them, but every camper had to have a hot meal. The kitchen staff always had a pot of boiling water on the stove, ready to whip up a plate of plain spaghetti. It was the counselors' responsibility to ensure that the boys ate properly. Dinner was more casual—sandwiches, hot dogs, light snacks—and it was popular among the boys.

After he finished playing the national anthem, David Cohen continued with soft, popular music until the main luncheon course plates were removed. He then shut the piano lid, cracked his knuckles, picked up the sheet music he'd brought, and retired to a place at one of the picnic tables in the back to take his meal with the maintenance workers and commissary staff.

Flowing in full caftan, Anthony Esposito sat with other staff members at one of the tables on the platform. Another of his demands was that he not be distracted at mealtime by a bunch of unruly young boys at the same table. Anthony Esposito was an interesting study himself, growing up in Pittsfield, Massachusetts, the only son of immigrant Italians who settled in western Massachusetts after World War I. Anthony's parents were caretakers for Zenas Crane Jr., a descendant of the Crane family, owners of the prestigious stationery empire located in nearby Dalton, Massachusetts.

Zenas Crane maintained two estates in Dalton. The main property was called "The Boulders," named appropriately since the facade of the mansion was covered in fieldstone and it was situated atop a steep hillside. The secondary residence was "Willow Brook," a Cottswold-style country cottage in the Berkshire foothills. The Espositos took care of both properties but spent most of their time at the Boulders, where they had a small suite of rooms off the kitchen.

Anthony's mother was the cook and head housekeeper, with two maids working under her; his father was the groundskeeper and general handyman. To supplement his income from Zenas Crane, Mr. Esposito was also a patternmaker, and he traveled extensively throughout New England selling his designs. Anthony's mother covered for her husband as well as she could when he was traveling, enlisting her son to do some of the lighter chores. Mr. Crane was aware of the situation but looked the other way since he liked the hardworking Italian family, and no one in the Berkshires could come close to matching Mrs. Esposito's secret recipe for strawberry shortcake.

Mrs. Esposito pulled her son out of the Pittsfield elementary public school system when he was in fifth grade. The teasing and bullying had become too painful, and when Anthony came home in tears one day with a bloody nose, she decided it was time to homeschool her child. Anthony had had a weight problem since he was born; doctors at the House of Mercy Hospital in Pittsfield diagnosed him with a thyroid condition, but neither medication nor a rigid diet proved effective in controlling his weight: Anthony was fat. The kids at school called him "dumbo" and "blubber boy," and teachers did little to discourage such behavior, dismissing it with a "kids will be kids" mentality.

Anthony flourished in the homeschool environment, spending hours studying in the Crane family library at the Boulders. It was there that he discovered his love for music. Zenas Crane was an opera buff and had a vast collection of rare 78 and 33 rpm records that Anthony carefully placed on the Harman Kardon turntable. Anthony listened to Puccini and Verdi for hours, dreaming one day of performing himself.

Every Saturday, Anthony faithfully tuned in to WGRS Radio from West Hartford to listen to the live broadcast from the Metropolitan Opera House sponsored by Texaco and narrated by Milton Cross.

As a patron of the Tanglewood Music Festival in nearby Lenox, Mr. Crane had season tickets that he rarely used. Aware of Anthony's keen interest in classical music, Mr. Crane often gave his tickets to the Espositos, who would take their son to listen to the Boston Symphony under the summer starlit skies of the Berkshires.

The State of Massachusetts Department of Education did not approve of Anthony's homeschool program and threatened to press charges of child neglect unless the boy was sent back to the public school system. But the months he had spent at home and the long hours studying in the Crane library had fortified Anthony, so he was more tolerant of the abuse he would face when he returned to public school.

Tim and Anthony Esposito got along quite well, spending at least two hours together every afternoon following lunch, planning the talent show and the big season-end production that many of the boys' parents would attend. David was present at these meetings, quietly taking notes and jotting down any detail that Anthony wanted taken care of. David was like a personal secretary to Anthony (although it was obvious their relationship was more than that), never questioning a request, no matter how seemingly absurd or unnecessary. One thing out of the ordinary Tim did notice was that no matter what was going on, David dropped everything at three o'clock and disappeared briefly, returning with a cup of water and a small white pill that Anthony quickly popped into his mouth and swallowed along with a dainty sip of water. Without missing a beat, Anthony would continue whatever he had been doing.

Tim was disappointed that he had no say in the content of the material that would be performed at camp that summer. Anthony and

David had worked all that out back at Oberlin and had even had the sheet music and scripts ordered and shipped ahead. Tim felt left out of the creative process, but that small slight was overcome when he realized he would be in charge of all production: sets, costumes, lighting, props, everything except directing the actors, and even then, Anthony would frequently ask Tim's opinion of the staging of some particular number.

Although Tim didn't volunteer an opinion, he was surprised that the material for the big production would be selections from the recent Broadway hit musical *Li'l Abner*. Tim had seen only the movie adaptation, but he knew the original production was controversial, making fun of hillbillies and featuring sexy bombshells like Edie Adams as Daisy Mae and Tina Louise as Appassionata Von Climax. Tim was having a hard time visualizing how this material was going to work performed by a bunch of rich Jewish boys in the middle of the New Hampshire woods. He later learned that Anthony knew someone in the Guild, supposedly a friend of the producers, who had agreed to release the material to Anthony without royalties as a favor, even though the musical was still a popular draw in summer stock and dinner theatres. Tim suspected that Anthony's ability to deliver this kind of high-profile material based on the widely popular Al Capp comic strip had impressed Drew enough for him to hire Anthony for the position at Camp Robin Hood. Drew had to know that many of the boys' parents would be impressed, although he had probably failed to take into consideration how few would be pleased to see their son play Daisy Mae in drag.

The theme for the annual talent show was far less controversial, and if anything, it was rather boring. Anthony had chosen the broad theme of "America the Beautiful." Participants in the competition, open to all staff members and campers, could choose their own material, provided David had or could locate the sheet music. But the entries were not required to be musical. They could be spoken word, scenes from plays, poetry, stand-up comedy, impersonations—almost anything within the realm of good taste was acceptable. Of course, Anthony had final approval of all material, seemingly to ensure that it fit the theme. But he was unlikely to reject any entry unless he felt the performer might embarrass himself.

By the third day of camp, everyone was settled into his new life for the next eight weeks. Some of the first-timers, mostly the younger Tinker-Pagers and Jugglers, who'd been outwardly homesick, staging crying tantrums and refusing to eat, quickly lost their angst when it came time to sign up for optional activities, which were numerous and varied. Sign-up sheets were posted on the main bulletin board outside the Social Hall for campers to enroll in any activities that interested them. Anthony and Tim were shocked when they went to collect the sign-up sheet for the drama workshop, which originally had included blank spaces for twenty campers. An extra page had been attached to the original. In total, fifty-two boys had signed up for drama. That was nearly a third of the campers enrolled at Robin Hood. Originally Tim and Anthony had been concerned about attracting *enough* boys to cover all the work required for the talent show and to cast and mount the final production. Now they had a small army of volunteers, each of whom would be given some task to perform, since at Camp Robin Hood, no boy was ever denied the opportunity to participate in an activity that he was interested in and physically capable of doing.

Although Anthony would never admit it, the overwhelming interest in the drama workshop was due in large part to Tim's popularity among the boys. In the few short days since camp had started, Tim had been immediately recognized as a "favorite" counselor. Partly it was his age proximity to many of the boys. But the bigger reason was his open friendliness to everyone and his willingness to help out in any situation, even those beyond his officially assigned responsibilities. Tim was in his element, surrounded by the warmth of a big family he had never experienced before.

After breakfast, campers were required to participate in some sort of team sport: softball, soccer, basketball, touch football—all competitive activities, but with no set teams. The boys could switch any day they wanted, so if they were not particularly adept at one sport or did not like the teammates they were paired with, they could change.

Following morning team sports, and weather permitting, all campers were required to have a daily supervised swim in Lake Ossipee. The boys were grouped according to ability, not by age or rank. All counselors were required to participate in and supervise this important activity. At the end of the summer, no boy would leave Camp Robin Hood without having acquired at least basic swimming capabilities.

The talent show, scheduled for the third Saturday in July, roughly midway through the season, went off better than anyone had expected. There were over thirty entries, most of them musical renditions of all-American favorites, with David patiently plugging away on the upright piano, trying hard not to look bored. The winning entry, by far the most popular and most enthusiastically received, was surprisingly not a musical selection. Four boys in the thirteen-year-old Lancer group had gotten together and constructed an eight-foot-high replica of Mount Rushmore. They had concealed their creation in an old barn behind the Social Hall used for storage by the commissary staff. With flour and water as glue, the boys had molded and pasted together paper cups, plates, and napkins to form their unusual sculpture. It was then whitewashed with a concoction of milk and sand to give it a stony luster. When the masterpiece was unveiled to the tune of "Stars and Stripes Forever," most people didn't immediately notice that the figure of Theodore Roosevelt had been transformed to the likeness of Andy Rabinowitz. Except for Andy's full beard, the two men bore a striking resemblance. As the audience began to catch on, roars of approval and cries of "It's Andy!" filled the great Social Hall. The four Lancers took a bow in front of a standing ovation, and no one was surprised when the boys walked off with first place in the talent contest.

The morning after the talent show, a Sunday, was Tim's birthday, a secret he had unsuccessfully tried to keep quiet. Aided by Mike Ross, as the rest of the campers slept in, the Jugglers in Robin's Roost pounced on Tim's bunk, wrestling him out from under the covers and pinning him facedown on the cabin floorboards with his hands and feet held tightly behind his back. Tim's resistance was more feigned than real because he knew the drill. Every counselor on his birthday got the traditional dunking in the lake. Led by Mike Ross, the six Jugglers dangled Tim by his hands and feet, dragged him to the end of the rowboat pier, and on the count of three hurled Tim into the frigid lake. The six Jugglers immediately jumped in behind Tim, taking turns trying to dunk him under the water. At that point a loud whistle sounded from the nearby shore, where Drew was standing with a number of boys from the neighboring cabins, awakened by the commotion, and had come to join in the party.

"C'mon, everybody out," Drew said good-naturedly. "You all know the rules."

Mike and a few other campers stood at the shore with dry towels as the birthday boy and his Juggler followers emerged from the lake, shivering in wet Jockey shorts.

"Tim, can I see you before you go up to breakfast?" Drew asked as Tim dried off on the shore.

"Sure," Tim replied, puzzled. "Is anything wrong?"

"No, nothing like that. Just something you and I have to talk about," Drew said vaguely. Then, turning back and smiling, he added, "Oh, and by the way, happy birthday!"

Drew was waiting for Tim on the veranda of the Social Hall when the boys filed in for breakfast. Putting his hand on Tim's shoulder, he broke the news that Anthony had been rushed to the hospital in North Conway shortly after midnight. He'd suffered a mild heart attack but was resting comfortably at the hospital. Unfortunately, Anthony would not be returning to camp to finish the season. The doctors had insisted he go back to Oberlin, where he would be closer to medical resources should he need them. Camp Robin Hood was far too remote a location for a heart patient. Drew explained that he and Tim would have to take over full responsibility for staging the final production of *Li'l Abner*, although David had agreed to stay on until the end of the summer to handle the music.

"I think he's happy to be away from 'Mother' for a while," Drew joked.

Tim smiled in agreement, although he was uncomfortable with Drew's familiarity.

Casting for *Li'l Abner*, the most difficult part of the undertaking, had already been completed a week before, and rehearsals had begun. Although Drew said he would be involved, it was left almost entirely up to Tim and David to get the show ready. The controversial part of Daisy Mae had been given to Jimmy Slatkin, a twelve-year-old Yeoman who had a full head of curly blond hair and an angel-like face. He was also the top athlete in his division, excelling at swimming, soccer, and baseball—in fact, there wasn't one sport that didn't seem to come naturally to Jimmy Slatkin. The part of Abner was given to Stu Abrams, who at 140 pounds was easily the most fully developed and muscular fourteen-year-old Friar there. The rest of the roles were divided among the boys who had signed up for the drama workshop and who wanted to perform besides helping with the sets and lighting. They made up an enthusiastic, if scruffy, bunch of "townspeople" and "hillbillies."

Anthony had cleverly taken the show's script and created a narrator (played by Mike Ross) who read the storyline aloud, as though telling the tale of Dogpatch and its quirky inhabitants. Anthony had been careful to edit out any risqué or satirically political elements. This format created opportunities to segue into musical numbers, while retaining the original comic-strip feel of the material. The show ran a little more than an hour, and it got a rousing reception from the parents who showed up to see it and from the audience of camp employees and their friends from Center Ossipee and North Conway.

Jimmy Slatkin's parents did attend and made a point, although briefly, of congratulating Tim on the success of the show and on their son's performance. The next day, the campers said tearful good-byes to the staff and vowed to see each other again next summer. Then the boys boarded the waiting yellow school buses that would take them to South Street Station or Logan Airport for the final trip home. Drew had offered Tim a ride back to Connecticut in the camp van the next day, to spare him the ordeal of riding a train for hours with a bunch of rambunctious young boys. That night, after sharing dinner with the few remaining staff who had gathered for a final farewell in Andy's cabin, Tim wrote the following letter while he was alone in Robin's Roost:

August 19, 1962

Dear Mr. and Mrs. Slatkin,

I'm sorry I didn't have the opportunity of talking to you more than I did while you were visiting camp, so I'll have to do it by mail now.

As you know, Jimmy played Daisy Mae in our production of "Li'l Abner." I don't have to tell you what a wonderful job he did because I'm sure you've heard this from other sources, but I would like to tell you why we selected Jimmy to play the part. Of course he had the singing and acting ability, but more important, he is a well-rounded boy, highly thought of by his fellow campers. We felt that a top athlete like Jimmy would not be subject to hazing for taking a girl's part, and fortunately this proved to be true. I know that it is hard, especially for a father, to be proud of his son playing a girl's part in a play, but I personally feel that what Jimmy accomplished on our stage is equal to any victory he has achieved on the athletic field.

I have worked with many campers this past summer and very few can compare with Jimmy as far as attitude, cooperation and ability. He was a pleasure to work with at all times. You have a son who reflects your fine training and one who is a credit to you as parents.

Thank you for giving me the opportunity of working with Jimmy, a boy who means a great deal to me, and one who makes the closing of camp so painful for me.

Very truly yours,

Tim Halladay
Assistant Drama Director

"Bejees, Hickey ... what'd you do to the booze?" Tim said with a laugh, taking a line from *The Iceman Cometh*. He crushed the empty Coke can he was holding and looked at the clock on the fireplace mantelpiece. It was almost six; he had been studying all afternoon, and he'd managed to read all of *The Iceman Cometh* and *Long Day's Journey into Night*, enough O'Neill for any sane person to digest in one afternoon. It was time for a quick shower, and then he'd join Blade for drinks and dinner, as he had promised.

A few minutes later, Tim stepped out of the shower and stood naked in the small apartment, towel-drying his hair. He looked again at the certificate Blade had framed, and he smiled. Below a picture of Andy shaking hands with Tim was the inscription "Counselor of the Year—Camp Robin Hood—Summer 1962." Tim had enjoyed that summer in New Hampshire and had become attached to the boys, who at various times had seemed like younger brothers to him. Dropping the towel to the floor, Tim lifted the framed citation off the wall, turned it over, and smiled as he traced his finger across the familiar double arches with dark egg-shaped eyes peering out and across the words crudely stenciled underneath: "Jeffrey Was Here."

CHAPTER 8

"Did you get a lot of studying done?" Blade asked, looking up from the crossword puzzle she'd been working on.

"I guess you could call it that, if spending all afternoon with a poet obsessed with death is studying," Tim said as he went to the sideboard where the bar had been set out. He poured himself a strong drink and, toasting his aunt, said again, "Bejees, Hickey ... what'd you do to the booze?"

"What?" Blade asked, befuddled. "Is something wrong?"

"No, just too much Eugene O'Neill," Tim offered without further explaining. "Thanks for getting Dewar's. You know how I hate that other swill you keep around for your guests who drink scotch."

"Scotch ... vile stuff, if you ask me. A true southern lady would never touch it," Blade said, sipping her Jim Beam bourbon.

"Since when did you become a southern lady?" Tim teased.

"Well, the District of Columbia is on the border, and I'm certainly more southern in my ways than our Yankee family up in Westport."

"Now, now. Let's be charitable," Tim laughed as he settled into the sofa opposite his aunt. Having drinks in the drawing room before dinner was a ritual they both enjoyed.

"Have you sent in your application to Yale?" Blade probed. It was a sensitive issue.

"I have all the papers filled out, but I haven't mailed them in yet."

"And the recommendation from Red? You are including that, aren't you?"

"Yes, of course," Tim answered, annoyed his aunt would bring up the subject.

"I mean, it should pull a lot of weight, considering …" Blade stopped short, realizing what she was saying.

"Blade … how could you?" Tim snapped, not trying to hide his distaste.

"Yes, of course," Blade said, retreating. "What was I thinking? But you know Red was very popular at Yale," she continued, not content to give up the subject completely.

Red Ryder had indeed been a popular and influential figure at Yale Drama School. Her father, Tom Ryder, had been a professor there for over twenty years, and although his glamorous daughter had never graduated, she had attended classes. She appeared for two summers at the Williamstown Theatre Festival, whose cofounder and artistic director, Nick Agropolis, was the head drama school professor at Yale. Red's father worked as his assistant every summer, turning out what many critics believed was some of the best theatre being done outside New York. Red was playing Madge in a production of *Picnic* when she was discovered by two producers who abruptly offered her the choice role of Janet Matthews in the new NBC soap opera *Another World*.

"You know, even if I am accepted," Tim said, turning the discussion away from Red and the glowing recommendation she'd written for him, "I'll never get a deferment."

"You're assuming you will be drafted," Blade said.

"Of course I'll be drafted. With the way things are going right now, it's a wonder they're even letting me finish at William and Mary.

Probably because they want all the college grads they can get to ship off to OCS," Tim said. "Officer's Candidate School," he explained, seeing his aunt didn't understand. "We've already gotten a pep talk from the ROTC guys on campus."

"Well, even if you are drafted, there's no guarantee they'll take you."

"There's nothing wrong with me, Aunt Blade." Tim bristled at even an oblique suggestion that his sexual orientation might be an issue with the military. He would rather be hanged than check the box admitting he had homosexual tendencies, or however the government phrased the question of whether or not you were queer.

An awkward pause filled the drawing room until Blade broke the silence. "Will you fix me another drink, Tim? I seem to have inhaled that one rather quickly."

"Sure," Tim said, relieved to be moving on. "Another Jim Beam for the southern lady?" he joked, taking his aunt's empty glass.

"Yes, and there's something I'd like to run by you."

"Shoot," Tim answered, knowing by her tone that his aunt was up to something. "I'm all ears."

"Well, I've been thinking of what to get you for graduation," she started, "but with all this uncertainty you seem to be creating about your draft status and graduate school ..."

Tim cut her off. "I'm not creating anything. Guys younger than me with no deferments are getting drafted every day. It's only a matter of time. Hell, I might as well enlist and get it over with."

"Stop talking silly, Tim. You're not going to join the army."

"No, but I might get lucky and get accepted into the air force or navy, but I understand the waiting lists for those branches are really long. Someone told me that it would be five years before the wimpy coast guard would even start considering new applications."

"So you're just going to sit by and see what happens?" Blade challenged.

"The King's Arms has agreed to let me stay on for the summer, even though I will have graduated." It was policy at Colonial Williamsburg that all waiters employed by the taverns in the historic district must be full-time students at the college. Tim had worked at the King's Arms

Tavern throughout his undergraduate days, and he'd risen to number two in seniority. There was only one law student who had worked there longer.

"And Harold has agreed to let me do *The Glory* as long as I'm available this summer, although I will just be a swing dancer and have some walk-on roles." Harold Spivey was the director of *The Common Glory*, the outdoor pageant by Paul Green, which played every summer in Williamsburg at the Lake Matoaka amphitheatre on the college campus. Spivey was also head of the William and Mary Theatre and Speech Department, and he had been impressed with Tim from the first time he'd come to audition for the department. Tim had become somewhat of a protégé of the professor when he was cast in the plum role of George Gibbs in *Our Town* his freshman year.

"I see you've got it all worked out," Blade said approvingly.

"Well, it's a short-term plan. I didn't spend four years in college hoping to be a waiter and a swing dancer."

"Of course, if you're accepted at Yale, which you almost certainly will be …"

"That's a big *if*," Tim said skeptically.

"Well, you'll know soon enough if you ever send in your application." Before Tim could respond to Blade's jab, she continued. "That works perfectly with my plan."

"Your plan?" Tim said suspiciously.

"Yes, I want to take you to South America as a graduation present."

"What?" Tim was used to almost anything from his aunt, but this had come out of nowhere.

"We can leave right after graduation and be gone for two weeks."

"But what about my job?"

"I'm certain the King's Arms can survive without you a few days, and that play doesn't open until late in June."

"But we have rehearsals," Tim started to object.

"Nonsense. You did that show last summer. How much rehearsal do you need? I'm sure Professor Spivey will work it out for you." Blade was aware of how fond the professor was of her nephew.

"I guess ..." Tim said, fumbling over his words.

"Then it's settled. We'll leave right after graduation. It will be late fall there, perfect cool weather. You're going to love Argentina. Joseph took me there on our honeymoon, and I have such fond memories," Blade reflected wistfully.

Indeed, it was in Buenos Aires that Blade had first made love to her husband—the first time she'd had sex with a man. Although Blade projected the persona of a liberal, free-spirited woman, she was, in reality, very conservative. Her Catholic upbringing at times made her feel more suited to life in a convent than to running a household and raising children. She never disclosed to her husband, during their brief marriage, that she could not conceive, an admission she was able to avoid because of his untimely death.

Blade began rhapsodizing on the wonders of Argentina and the glorious time they would have there. Actually, the thought was appealing to Tim. He'd always hoped to travel to South America.

"Blade, you are something else." Tim smiled, in full submission now, and got up to give his aunt a hug.

"I'm making arrangements with people in the travel department at the Archives. Betina is friendly with them, and they do travel arrangements for diplomats and other bigwigs on the Hill."

"I'm sure it will be first-class," Tim acknowledged.

"Well, it will be comfortable," Blade said with a wink, settling the issue. "Are you hungry? Mattie made a roast, which is in the oven now."

Mattie Rawlings had worked for the Anthony family for years. She'd started as a cleaning lady when Blade was a little girl, and she'd eventually become a live-in maid who did the cooking as well. For many years she had lived in the basement apartment now occupied by Tim. When their parents died, Blade and her sister Betina assumed responsibility for running the house and asked Mattie to stay on. However, when Blade married and Joseph moved into the house, he wasn't comfortable with someone else living under the same roof, full-time. Betina had already moved out, and Joseph wanted privacy with his new bride, so Mattie was forced to move in with her daughter, a single mom raising a young son. Over the years, and after Joseph's death, Mattie's role was reduced to cooking for Blade's social events and coming in once a week to do light housekeeping. Her grandson Duane, who was now a teenager, helped her with the cleaning, hauling the vacuum cleaner up and down the three flights of stairs in the narrow townhouse. Although he was underage, Duane also served as the bartender at Blade's social gatherings, perfecting and serving her famous "Bottoms Up" concoction. This lethal combination was an "eye-opener" reserved for Sunday brunch: a frosted, double old-fashioned glass was filled with fresh grapefruit juice, into which a chilled jigger of bourbon was dropped. The recipient had to raise the double glass, toast the other guests "bottoms up," and drink in one continuous gulp. As the glasses tilted, the bourbon and grapefruit juice mixed, giving an instant blast. If the drinker hesitated, the glasses would tumble and spill out into an unsightly mess.

"Is Duane coming to help out tomorrow?" Tim asked when they sat at the dining room table.

"Yes, although it's a small group. I don't like people having to make their own drinks."

"He must be quite a young man now."

"He'll be entering Howard University this fall," Blade said. "Mattie is beside herself. You know how she dotes on that boy."

"Yes, I always thought he was a good kid."

"Are you going out tonight?" Blade probed.

"Yes, I've had enough O'Neill for one day. I'll work on the paper when I get back to Williamsburg. You know, I'm going to have to leave right after brunch tomorrow. I have a ton of work to catch up on."

"Yes, of course," Blade agreed, but she sounded disappointed. She always dreaded her nephew's leaving to go back to school. "Then South America is settled?" Blade interjected, not wanting the conversation to end.

"I guess." Tim smiled, knowing the issue had been settled before they even had the discussion. "Who's going to tell Mom?"

"I'll take care of your mother. She won't give me a hard time. Why should she?" Blade reasoned.

"Fine. You handle her," Tim said, getting up to clear his plate. "Don't wait up for me tonight. I may be late."

"Don't worry. I'll be in bed long before you get in. I have guests coming in the morning, remember."

"What time?" Tim asked, as if it mattered.

"I said at eleven, but you know what that means. I thought we'd eat by one. Does that give you enough time?" Blade asked, concerned.

"I'll make it work," Tim said, giving his aunt a kiss on the cheek. "I can always slip out if I have to."

"I've asked JoEllen to come," Blade said hesitantly. "I hope you don't mind."

"No, not at all," Tim said, unsurprised, having heard this from Father Hartwell already. "JoEllen and I are good friends. We have no issues."

"She's bringing her fiancé, or whatever he is. The young man she's living with."

"Should be interesting." Tim smiled and then bounded down the stairs to change for his night out.

The weather had turned warm and humid, and all that was left of the morning's snow-dusting was slick dew that made the leaf-strewn cobblestones slippery. It was a short walk to the Tombs, where a line had already formed on the stairway leading to the underground tavern. Tim took his place, and after about fifteen minutes, the line inched toward the entrance door. There he paid his two-dollar cover fee and pushed his way through the cave-like bar, which smelled of stale beer with a suggestion of urine. Cigarette smoke burned his eyes as he looked around to see if he recognized anyone. The crowd on Saturday night was different from the regulars who frequented during the week: these were mostly kids from Virginia and Maryland who came into DC to party on weekends. Tim twisted his way to the bar to order a beer, but it was futile. He couldn't get the frazzled bartender's attention, so he just wormed his way back up the crammed stairwell and out into the humid night air.

He decided to check out the Cellar Door a few blocks down the hill on M Street, to see if the phenomenal new singer Roberta Flack was performing. She was, but according to the chalkboard sign outside the door, her next set was not until eleven, almost an hour away. The line at the Cellar Door was even longer than at the Tombs, and Tim was not in the mood to play the sardine game and listen to yet another rendition of "The First Time."

It was too early to go home; Blade would still be up watching the news. Tim felt the Volkswagen key in the pocket of his parka; he'd had the foresight to take his car keys with him when he left the apartment earlier in the evening. He turned and climbed the cobblestone hill up to Thirty-Third Street. The VW was parked in the alley behind the house, so he could retrieve the car without raising his aunt's suspicion about why he was taking it out so late.

Tim was fairly certain that he could find the warehouse bar in Foggy Bottom where the student from Georgetown had taken him. He wasn't concerned sbout the police taking down his license number and possibly giving him a ticket. The Volkswagen was registered in his mother's name in Connecticut, and it wouldn't be the first time she'd received a citation from some out-of-state law enforcement agency.

After a few wrong turns, Tim finally saw a few dark town cars parked in the block ahead, with their drivers either behind the wheel or standing clustered in small groups, smoking cigarettes, obviously waiting. As he drew closer, he saw more cars, parked erratically on the sidewalk or blocking driveways. It was as though the drivers had abandoned their cars in haste.

Tim parked in front of a boarded-up industrial building a few blocks away and walked determinedly to the unmarked entrance of the warehouse club. He paid the ten-dollar cover fee (twice what he remembered), and then he was inside the sprawling open space. A live band was playing deafening rock music from a makeshift stage at the far end of the building. It was still early, but the place was already packed with boys dancing, their shirts off, under brilliant, flashing strobe lights. The aroma of poppers permeated the air, barely covering the sweet smell of marijuana. Even for a private, after-hours club, the atmosphere was boldly permissive: open containers of alcohol were apparent everywhere amid a crowd of young men who looked mostly below the legal drinking age of twenty-one.

Tim found his way to the bar and ordered a beer, which cost another two dollars; drinks were not included tonight in the cover charge. As he wedged his way to lean against the bar, Tim noticed a lithe boy dressed only in white Jockey shorts, socks, and tennis shoes, prancing up and down the bar to the delight of patrons who were lined up and waving dollar bills to attract his attention. When a larger denomination, like a five- or ten-dollar bill, found its way into the fray, the boy would stop, lean down provocatively, and pluck the bill from the holder's outstretched hand. This met with loud approval from the crowd, who cheered the boy on as he placed the bill under the elastic strip of his Jockey shorts. Tim remembered from his previous visit that as the money increased, so did the sexy activity. The men participating in this game were largely older and well dressed, presumably the ones whose drivers waited outside. They'd not come here to dance and sniff poppers with the guys gyrating beneath strobe lights on the dance floor. Tim thought a few of the men looked familiar, but it was hard to see in the dimly lit bar, filled as it was with smoke and flashing lights. The owners made sure that an air of anonymity prevailed throughout the club, to protect their valued clients' privacy. These were some of the same men who ensured that law enforcement officers assigned to patrol the area had been chosen based on their dedication to serving individuals who held public office and sat on influential committees.

Tim was squirming against two guys wedged next to him at the bar, attempting to order another beer, when he felt a tap on his shoulder.

"I see you found it," a familiar voice said. Tim turned to face the young, blond Georgetown student who had first brought him to the club a few weeks earlier.

"Fancy meeting you here!" Tim was happy to see someone he knew.

"Let me get that," the student said, pushing Tim's money back into his hand. "They take my coupons here."

"You come here a lot?" Tim joked. "Looks like they know you."

"My second home," he said, handing Tim a fresh beer.

"Thanks," Tim said. "Uh, I think I forgot your ..."

"No, you didn't. We never introduced ourselves last time. As I remember, you couldn't wait to get out of here," the student teased. "I'm Emerson. But my friends just call me M."

"Nice to finally meet you," Tim said, extending his hand. "I'm ..."

"I know. You're Tim!" M said, cutting him off. "I've seen you at the Tombs, and I asked around."

"Oh." Tim was caught off guard, but he was flattered too.

"Let's move back from the bar before it gets too crazy," M suggested.

"Too crazy?"

"Yes! Tonight is Jingle Balls."

"Jingle Balls?" Tim repeated stupidly.

"Didn't you see the flyer going around?"

"What flyer?"

"Never mind. You'll get the gist of it quick enough," M smirked.

The boy who'd been dancing on the bar was now joined by five others, all six now wearing jockstraps with ten- and twenty-dollar bills tucked under the elastic bands. The music intensified, and the lights dimmed throughout the bar; the boys were illuminated by spotlights following them as they pranced and strutted provocatively up and down the bar top. The lineup at the bar had shifted and was now almost exclusively men in dark suits who were studying the proceedings with the intensity and seriousness of high-rolling bettors at a racetrack.

"Here," M said, slipping a wrinkled piece of paper into Tim's hand. "Tonight's holiday menu."

Tim looked at the well-worn paper and in the dim light could make out under a heading of "Jingle Balls" what looked like a parody of Christmas carols—and a price list. Before the paper was snatched out of his hand by an aggressive leather-man, Tim made out selections like "I'm Creaming for a White Christmas—$100" and "A Lay in a Manger (takeout)—$500."

"The owners know this is probably the last weekend before they're busted, so they're letting it all hang out," M explained to a speechless Tim. The action along the bar had heated up, with many ten-dollar bills in the air and an occasional jockstrap lowered to reveal a full erection. At the far end of the bar, one of the boys was prone, with a dark suit hovering over him, as a drunken, rowdy crowd shoved around to watch.

"Looks like one of the holiday specials is being delivered," M said snidely. Turning to Tim, he asked directly, "Do you like watching?"

Trying not to blush, Tim responded, "I find the humiliation kind of interesting."

"I'll show you some humility," M said unexpectedly, and putting his hand on the back of Tim's neck, he pulled him forward and kissed him on the lips. Although surprised, Tim did not resist. "What say we go somewhere and have some holiday fun of our own?" M added.

"What do you have in mind?"

"Well, my dorm's a bit crowded ..." M started.

"I'm parked outside. We can go to my place," Tim said.

"Where's that?"

"I stay with my aunt in Georgetown."

"Convenient!" M gripped Tim's hand. "You drove? No cab?"

Once outside, they walked by a tangle of double-parked cars and past streams of guys heading toward the warehouse. M had one arm across Tim's shoulder, hugging him close. They found the Volkswagen in a few minutes, and when Tim unlocked the car, M kissed him again, lingering as he pressed their bodies against the car door.

"You're something else," Tim said approvingly.

M confessed, "I was hoping I'd run into you tonight."

The ride back to Thirty-Third Street was stop-and-go because of the Saturday night traffic. M cradled Tim's hand whenever he shifted the car into gear. At last, Tim edged the VW into the alleyway behind his aunt's townhouse.

"This is where you stay?" M asked, impressed.

"I have the basement apartment."

"How convenient," M said. "How very convenient."

Inside the small apartment, the boys embraced and exchanged a long, passionate kiss. M ran his hands inside Tim's parka, gently massaging his lower back and then moving to his chest. Tim could feel the first button of his shirt being opened as he gently pulled back.

"Hey, tiger! What's the hurry?" Tim said good-naturedly, slowly slipping out of his jacket and then taking M's off. He got beer from the small refrigerator and ignited a Presto-log in the fireplace, after which the two curled up on the small sofa.

Tim explained that he was a senior at William and Mary and that whenever he came up to DC on weekends, he stayed here.

"And your aunt is cool with …"

"She's very cool," Tim assured him.

M was a freshman at Georgetown. He'd moved to DC from Argentina, which he'd left because of the oppressive dictatorship of Juan Carlos Onganía. The military government had raided the University of Buenos Aires in the famous *La Noche de los Bastones Largos*, a protest that would become a war cry for young intellectuals. It was the start of a brain drain on the cultural and academic community in Argentina, forcing many professors and students to leave the country.

M was born in Atlanta, which explained the slight southern accent, but his father, a senior marketing executive for the international division of Coca-Cola, moved around a lot. They'd lived in Spain a few years while his father supervised the opening of a bottling plant outside Madrid, but for the last few years his family had been living in Argentina.

"My aunt wants to take me to Argentina as a graduation present."

"You'll love it," M said. "It's not like any place in South America. It looks kind of French—at least Buenos Aires does—but it's very Italian. If that makes any sense." He then stared at Tim for a moment before asking, "Are you sure you've never been to BA?"

"No. Why do you ask?"

"I don't know. You just look so … oh, what the fuck!" By this time M had loosened Tim's belt buckle and had undone the first button on his jeans. Tim didn't resist and instead lay back on the sofa as M methodically removed the rest of Tim's clothes, down to his Jockey shorts. M stood and shed his own clothes into a pile on the floor. The two stood and embraced before the flickering Presto-log and then inched slowly toward the nearby bed.

Tim looked across the covers at the alarm clock on the night table: it was almost six o'clock. M lay curled up under Tim's right arm, his blond head resting peacefully on Tim's chest. He was purring gently like a contented cat. Not wanting to disturb his guest, Tim pulled the comforter up over both of them and settled back into the warmth of their embrace. They could sleep at least another two hours before Tim had to get up and think about his aunt's brunch.

The sound of footsteps above them in the kitchen woke Tim abruptly. It must have been Mattie and Duane getting ready. The bedside clock now read a little after nine; it was later than Tim had intended to sleep. He slowly withdrew his arm from under M's shoulder and gently brushed the light shock of hair from across M's forehead and out of his eyes.

"Hey, sleepy. Time to wake up." Tim softly tapped M's shoulder and brushed a kiss along his cheek.

"Jingle Balls?" M said devilishly through half-open eyes.

"Not now," Tim laughed, squashing a pillow over his friend's head. "Time to get up."

"No more Christmas songs?" M joked, acting disappointed.

"No more Christmas songs … at least not for now." Tim pulled the covers off his guest, who was obviously still ready to play. "Want to take a shower?"

"All right." M sleepily slid out of the bed, naked. "Be like that."

Tim directed M to the shower and pulled a fresh towel off the hook on the back of the door. M draped the towel over his head and sauntered suggestively into the bathroom. As Tim was putting on water for instant coffee, he smiled; he had never met anyone quite so uninhibited as M.

"Find everything you need?" Tim asked when M emerged, still dripping, from the bathroom.

"You're very well equipped," M said flirtatiously, still ready to play.

After M finished the now cold instant coffee, he put on his parka and was getting ready to leave when Tim unexpectedly asked, "Do you speak Spanish?"

"Enough to get by," M responded.

"Do you know a five-letter word for a cold period in Spain?"

"Huh?" M asked, confused by the unusual question.

"A five-letter word for a cold period in Spain," Tim repeated.

M thought for a second, looking at his friend strangely, and then answered. "I guess *enero* would work."

"*Enero?*"

"Yes. *E-n-e-r-o*. It means January in Spanish. You could call that a cold period in Spain."

"That's it!" Tim beamed. "*Enero!*"

CHAPTER 9

Mattie Rawlins and her grandson Duane had commandeered the kitchen in preparation for brunch. Duane had temporarily emptied the freezer of all frozen vegetables, filling it with double old-fashioned glasses and two bottles of bourbon for the famous Bottoms Up drinks. He'd squeezed two large pitchers of fresh grapefruit juice, which Blade insisted on using instead of that mixture from a concentrate can.

"Looks like everything's under control," Tim said as he poked his head in through the kitchen door. He picked up one of the Virginia ham biscuits cooling on the counter.

"You want a Bottoms Up, Mr. Tim?" Duane offered.

"Not today, Duane. I'm driving back to Williamsburg this afternoon. It'll just make me sleepy."

Popping the biscuit into his mouth, Tim said, "By the way, I hear you're going to Howard this fall."

"Yes, I got an early acceptance."

"He's going to be studying premed," Mattie added proudly.

"Great," Tim said. "That's a tough major, but I'm sure you'll do fine."

Pushing Tim away from the cooling biscuits, Mattie said, "Go in there and see if your Aunt Blade needs anything. We have lots of work to do in here."

Blade was standing in the center of the drawing room as Tim approached to give her a kiss on the cheek. She was doing her last walk-through to make sure everything was in place before her guests arrived. Cupping a Paperwhite Narcissus cluster sprouting from one of the pots that Tim had arranged around the room, Blade inhaled deeply.

"The fragrance is so heavenly," she murmured, closing her eyes. "It's almost erotic."

"Innocent, I think, is the word," Tim corrected.

"Yes, of course," Blade agreed, opening her eyes. "Innocent." After pausing a moment to take the perfumed blossom in her palm, she turned to her nephew, "Why not mix in some daffodils for color once in a while, especially in these dreary winter months? Some yellow might be cheerful."

"Daffodils are for staying outside, like guard soldiers. Their trunks are too imposing to mix with narcissus. Besides, they smell like men's talcum. They're definitely only for outdoors."

Blade knew better than to argue with Tim when it came to flowers, particularly when it came to his precious Paperwhite Narcissus.

"Who was that young man I saw leaving by the back gate earlier?" Blade asked matter-of-factly.

"That was Emerson, a friend of mine from Georgetown," Tim said, not surprised by his aunt's observation. "He's an interesting young man. Just moved here from Argentina to start at Georgetown."

"Argentina?" Blade's interest was piqued. "You should have asked him to stay for brunch."

Tim quickly thought up an excuse. "He had to study."

"Maybe next time," Blade pushed. "Argentina! My! My!"

"I'll ask him next time," Tim said, letting the subject of his overnight guest drop.

The doorbell rang promptly at 11:00 a.m.: Father Hartwell, always the first to arrive to see if he could help Blade with the guest list or with any last-minute arrangements. He could be more efficient than a wedding planner.

The guests started to arrive. Two scholastics from Georgetown, young Jesuits who were studying to be priests but had not yet taken their final vows, were ushered in by Father Hartwell, as if he were taking them under his protective wing into a threatening environment. He introduced them to Tim. "This is Jim Benson, who's joined us from Boston College. His buddy is Jack LaGrange from Fairfield." The senior Jesuit dropped priestly nomenclature in making introductions, creating a sense of informality among the three young men. Although they were dressed in white collars and black suits, they seemed more like students than priests. As part of their training for the priesthood, they'd been given undergraduate teaching assignments at Georgetown.

Duane brought in a tray of Bottoms Up drinks, which he offered to the bemused Jesuits.

"Part of the initiation into my Aunt Blade's salon," Tim joked. "The trick is to drink it in one quick gulp. Don't stop halfway through, or you'll end up with a mess." Tim left the Jesuits fiddling with their drinks and worked his way back to the front door, where JoEllen was standing. She was loosening her scarf and removing her gloves when Tim tapped her on the shoulder.

"Hi, JoEllen," he said softly.

She turned, and when she saw it was Tim, she wrapped her arms around him in a tight embrace. "Oh, Tim," she said, "I was hoping you'd be here." She buried her head in Tim's shoulder, continuing to hold him close to her. After a long pause she stepped back to look at him. "How are you doing?" she asked with concern as she brushed strands of her loose hair from his blue blazer. It was the first time the two had spoken since Red's death.

"I'm okay," Tim responded somewhat unconvincingly. "You know ..." He held back the emotions that he was determined not to show.

"Tim, this is Frank," JoEllen said, drawing her fiancé into the conversation. "I think you two may have met at Olney."

"I'm sure we did," Tim said, shaking Frank's hand. They had met the summer Red was playing Cleopatra, when Tim came backstage with the bouquet of white flowers for the Queen of the Nile. It was the same summer Tim had started dating JoEllen, unaware that JoEllen and Frank were already considered a couple. Frank deLong was managing director of Olney, a position he still held in addition to being associate drama director at Catholic University. Frank knew that Tim was one of several young men JoEllen had flirtations with, but he'd looked the other way. It was a convenient arrangement since JoEllen and Frank enjoyed the company of some of the same boys, although Tim was not one of those.

Frank was a wiry, unattractive, lizard-like man in his midthirties, with a small, trim mustache and slicked-back hair, which looked like it rarely saw shampoo. His name, deLong, was an accurate descriptor, Tim had heard, which for many of the boys was his main attraction.

Duane arrived with the obligatory tray of Bottoms Up drinks, which both JoEllen and Frank took, already familiar with the ritual.

"Not for you today?" Frank teased when Tim passed on the strong drink.

"Driving back to Williamsburg this afternoon. Not a good idea to drink."

Frank drifted off to mingle with other guests, focusing on the two scholastics who didn't know anyone in the room. This left Tim and JoEllen some time alone.

"It must be really hard for you," JoEllen said, putting a hand on Tim's arm.

"I went to the Mass at St. Patrick's, which was quite a production," Tim said. "Then I went to Arlington on Friday, although burial was closed to the public. I stood on the hillside and watched. Of course, Hartwell was there, filling in for the archbishop."

"Hartwell wouldn't miss that for the world," JoEllen smirked.

"We had lunch after the service. I gave him a ride back from the cemetery, and we went to 1789."

"I'm surprised you were up to that," JoEllen said with a frown. "I thought you couldn't stand him."

"We have issues, but maybe it's time to move on."

"Do you think he really slept with Red?" JoEllen asked in her disarmingly direct way.

"What?" Tim blurted out, shocked.

"Isn't that the issue between you two?" JoEllen pressed.

"Fuck, no! What does it matter now anyway?"

Tim and JoEllen had never discussed his suspicion that the pompous Jesuit and the radiant actress had at some point had an affair, even though it was a prime topic of gossip in the Georgetown social set.

"So when are you and Frank getting married?" Tim asked, changing the subject.

"Probably after I graduate in June," JoEllen said noncommittally. "There's no rush since we're already living together."

"And you're doing Olney again this summer?"

"Unless something better comes up."

"Knowing you, it will."

"And you?" JoEllen teased, touching Tim's shirt collar.

"Everyone's pressing me to apply to Yale, but I keep telling them I'll never get a deferment. No one seems to listen or want to understand."

"So are you just going to wait until they haul you off to Vietnam?"

"It's not like that," Tim said defensively.

"I know." JoEllen pursed her lips to kiss Tim gently. "Let's go down to the greenhouse," JoEllen said. "We need to get away from the Bottoms Up crowd for a while."

Brunch was in full swing, with people beginning to feel the effects of the free-flowing alcohol. Conversation had risen to a boisterous level in the drawing room, and Blade was floating like a hummingbird from guest to guest, so no one noticed when Tim and JoEllen disappeared downstairs.

"So this is where you force the bulbs," JoEllen said as she slid her hand under Tim's blazer, kissing him on the lips.

"Hey, you're engaged." Tim pulled back.

"I know," she shrugged. "So what?"

JoEllen had first suspected Tim was gay soon after they started dating, but then so were a lot of the other guys she went out with. She got a strange thrill from seducing gay boys, and in truth, the sex was good. She didn't have to worry about faking an orgasm because once her partner had come, it was over.

"We did have fun," JoEllen said, tracing her index finger across Tim's upper lip, "even though we both knew it would never work."

Tim smiled. "Yeah."

"Remember when I took you to the Sands in Wilmington? I knew then." JoEllen said, referring to the drag club she had taken Tim to on their first date. From the outside, the Sands wasn't a place Tim would ever be drawn to.

"Don't worry," JoEllen had said that night, sensing Tim's hesitation. "The kids from Olney love this place, and the show is pretty special."

"What show?"

"You'll see," JoEllen laughed. "Don't be so uptight."

Inside, the bar was filled with a crowd of bikers and butch-looking girls. JoEllen waved to a waiter who obviously knew her, and he led them to a small table by a stage with a silver tinsel curtain.

"Is Mary here tonight?" JoEllen asked when the waiter placed two beers and a plastic bowl of peanuts on the table.

"You're in luck. Both Mary and Mariland are here tonight. Should be a great show."

JoEllen winked at Tim, toasting him with a stein of beer. "We're in luck," JoEllen repeated, mimicking the waiter. "They're both here tonight."

Tim was totally lost, but he was open to anything JoEllen might have had in mind; she was obviously in control of the evening. Before they'd finished their beers, another round arrived, and then the lights dimmed in the bar. A spotlight illuminated an easel placed on the stage in front of the silver tinsel curtain. In flowery lettering outlined in glitter, the poster read, "Mary Go Round performing selections from *Carousel*." A respectful hush came over the bar crowd as the spot faded on the easel before it was quickly swept off the stage. The tinsel curtain squeaked open. Faint sounds of the "Carousel Waltz" grew louder from a boom box placed onstage, and then a frail young dancer *en pointe* pirouetted gracefully in circles around the stage in perfect rhythm to the complex music. Obviously well trained in classical ballet, the dancer was a pretty young boy, at most sixteen years old. He wore white tights and a flimsy gauze blouse wrap that barely covered his slim body. The effect was to make him asexual, neither male nor female, a butterfly floating across the tacky stage in a smoke-filled bar. The audience of beer-drinking bikers seemed mesmerized by the beauty and grace of the young performer, who never slipped out of character or made eye contact with the audience. A hush fell over the room when he danced to the tune and lyrics of "When I Marry Mr. Snow." There was not a hint of a snicker from anyone in the saloon. The entire set lasted twenty minutes, and when he was taking his bow, to the strains of "You'll Never Walk Alone," there were howls of approval from the audience.

"You know I danced in *Carousel* my senior year at Elkton High," JoEllen reminded Tim. "But this boy is better than I ever hope to be. I knew when I first saw him that my career was not going to be in dance, a disappointment, I'm sure, for Arianna, who worked so hard with me all through high school. I didn't have half the talent that this young boy has," JoEllen said reflectively.

The lights came up in the bar as Mary Go Round finished her act and collected dollar bills tossed onstage in appreciation, a small reward for all the years of preparation and hours of work that had gone into that performance. The boy would soon realize the limitations of being a drag performer in a Delaware saloon. The easel reappeared onstage with a card listing the next act as "Song Stylings of Mariland Monroe," who had now become a favorite at the Sands. JoEllen knew Mariland as Johnnie Izzo from Elkton, but she had never acknowledged him by his real name when he was in drag.

"This next guy is really good," JoEllen said, clasping Tim's arm as the waiter brought a full pitcher of beer. "A sad product of Elkton who will probably never escape the town."

"You mean you know this kid?" Tim asked, astonished. JoEllen just smiled. "You never fail to amaze me," Tim said as the lights dimmed in the roadhouse saloon and Mariland Monroe appeared onstage. This was not your typical Judy Garland-type gay female impersonator with exaggerated makeup and a campy wig. The boy looked like the real Marilyn Monroe. He was beautiful and feminine, and when he sang "Little Girl Blue," the crowd of bikers stood reverently, ready to protect this angel who'd mysteriously fallen into their den. When Mariland sang the lyrics "count your little fingers," JoEllen became emotional, and she held Tim's hand tightly.

"I think I've had enough of the Sands," she said, kissing Tim on the cheek. The two left money on the table for the beer and slipped a five-dollar bill on the stage, where Mariland was breaking into her rendition of "Happy Days Are Here Again."

In the parking lot outside, they barely had time to get into the VW before their hands were fumbling and unbuttoning each other's clothes. Tim's jeans were down to his knees, and JoEllen's panties were just loose enough for Tim to insert a finger. It was a clumsy mess later when the two tried to reconstruct themselves for the ride back to Olney.

Now, JoEllen and Tim stood in the greenhouse overlooking the pots of bulbs Tim had planted earlier that weekend. Laughter from the brunch crowd upstairs intruded on the tranquil mood as early afternoon sunlight filtered through the glass panes of the greenhouse.

"You knew I was gay from the beginning, didn't you?" Tim looked at JoEllen directly.

"We'd better be getting back upstairs before your aunt sends out the fire brigade to rescue us," JoEllen said, avoiding his question.

"Or put out the fire," Tim teased, kissing JoEllen tenderly.

When they returned to the gathering, no one seemed to notice Tim and JoEllen had been gone over an hour. Her fiancé, Frank, was still busy conversing with the two Jesuit scholastics; a young African poet, dressed in her native costume, was reading to an enraptured audience assembled in a small group at the fireplace. Duane had replaced the tray of Bottoms Up drinks with flutes of champagne and glasses of white wine, and he was passing them among the crowd of already relaxed guests.

"John, I don't suppose you've had a chance to talk to Tim," Blade said, tugging gently on Father Hartwell's sleeve.

"No, I haven't. The time didn't seem right. Besides, he's been with JoEllen ever since she arrived," the priest commented wryly.

"I noticed that."

"I assume you're talking about the graffiti thing," the priest said.

"Yes. But I agree. This probably isn't the best time to get into that."

"Perhaps you should just let it go," the Jesuit suggested.

The kitchen door opened as Mattie and Duane brought out two steaming trays to place in chafing dishes set up on the sideboard. Blade's brunch menu was always the same: chicken and dumplings in one tray and scrambled eggs with stewed tomatoes and okra in the other. Side dishes included Chesapeake Bay crab cakes, Virginia ham biscuits, frozen fruit salad, and Sally Lunn bread. Although brunch was buffet-style, Blade had Duane set up several folding chairs and small tables in the drawing room as guests were serving themselves, so that everyone would have a place to sit while eating. Blade's guests would never have to navigate through the challenge of balancing a plate of food in one hand and a drink in another while standing up, trying to engage in conversation.

"Aren't you two going to eat?" Blade asked, approaching Tim and JoEllen.

"Let me find Frank and get us a plate," JoEllen smiled. "Everything looks wonderful, Blade. As always."

"So when is the date?" Father Hartwell asked JoEllen, interjecting himself into the conversation. "I understand that you and Frank are engaged."

"Yes, Father," JoEllen said. "But we haven't set a date."

"I guess congratulations are in order just the same," the priest offered.

"Thank you," JoEllen answered politely. "But there's really no hurry, since I finish my master's in June, and then we still have the summer at Olney. After that, we'll have to see where we are."

"I think you want to rescue Frank from the two scholastics," Tim said to JoEllen, diplomatically ending the sensitive discussion of her engagement. Father Hartwell looked miffed at being cut off, but Tim continued. "Thanks again for lunch on Friday. I hadn't been to the 1789 in a long time. The Tombs doesn't really count," Tim joked, referring to the college hangout in the basement of the famous restaurant.

It was after three o'clock when the first guests began to leave, and only long after coffee and pecan bars had been set out.

"I'd better think about getting on the road," Tim said as he stood up and put his plate and napkin on the sideboard. "Sunday traffic's always heavy, and I need to get back"

"I know," Blade said, disappointed yet resigned. "I always dread this."

"I'll be back for New Year's, in a few weeks," Tim said apologetically. "I'm sure you have festivities planned." He kissed his aunt good-bye. Then turning to JoEllen he said, "Great to see you. And Frank, I'm sorry we didn't have more time to talk."

Tim was in the doorway leading to the basement apartment when he abruptly turned and called out to Blade, "*Enero.* That's the word."

Blade and the others looked perplexed as Tim laughed, realizing that no one, not even his aunt, knew what he was talking about. "*Enero. E-n-e-r-o.* A five-letter word for a cold period in Spain. *Enero.*"

"Oh, Tim … you're wonderful!" Blade said, smiling and delighted.

CHAPTER 10

Tim turned onto Key Bridge, heading toward Arlington Cemetery. He wasn't sure he would stop, but just in case, he had picked a small bunch of budding Paperwhite Narcissus in the greenhouse before leaving Thirty-Third Street. The fragile blooms lay innocently on the backseat of the old VW as though being kidnapped. He circled the roundabout at the end of the bridge, passing the off-ramp for the cemetery once, and then circled around again before deciding to turn off. The gravel roadway was familiar since he had been there just forty-eight hours before. The rows of stone markers stood stoically, silently honoring the soldiers buried below. Not far up the hillside, the eternal flame burned at the Kennedy memorial.

Tim pulled the VW to the side of the road and turned off the ignition, conscious that the whirring and clicking of the engine was an intrusion on the tranquil surroundings. He took the flowers from the backseat and walked the short distance up the hill to the fresh gravesite.

He was amazed to see that the stone marker was already in place: "Sarah Anne Ryder, Connecticut, 1ˢᵗ LT WAC, Jul 21, 1929–Nov 26, 1966."

He placed the small bouquet of narcissus in front of the marker and on top of the loose dirt where grass would eventually grow. It was against regulations to leave flowers or other decorations in the cemetery, but he knew Red would smile at the incursion of the little white flowers. Since it was Sunday, the groundskeepers would not come by at least until tomorrow, so Tim's small offering might survive a night with his beloved friend. He stood, hands folded before him, looking across the rolling hillside that ended with the Potomac in the distance.

Traffic on the interstate heading south toward Richmond was heavy, as expected on a Sunday afternoon, so Tim had to be alert. The old VW could hardly maintain the speed limit of fifty-five miles an hour; the car swayed like a leaf in the wind whenever big eighteen-wheelers whooshed by, forcing Tim to hold the steering wheel tight just to stay in his lane. He was relieved when, just before the Richmond city limit, the sign for the Williamsburg cutoff came into view. The final fifty miles of his trip back to campus would be less stressful on the two-lane country road, with its much lighter traffic and few big trucks.

It was after eight when Tim got back to his dorm. As a senior, he qualified for a single room, so he didn't have a roommate to contend with, but he still hated living in college-provided housing. Even with his own room, there was little privacy. Tim winced whenever he thought of how he'd had to be picked up off the hallway floor near the pay phone where he had collapsed upon hearing the news of Red's death. He was sure the two hunky frat guys had told everyone about the incident. Tim was on the waiting list for off-campus housing, but there were few approved apartments in the small historic town, and now, with only one semester left until he graduated, it seemed pointless to hope something might become available.

He switched on the light in his room and stepped over a pile of notices and papers that had been shoved under his door while he was away. He'd been gone less than a week, but a lot of junk mail, including the college newspaper, *The Flat Hat*, had accumulated. He picked up the pile of papers and tossed them on the bed along with his duffel bag. He unwrapped the roast beef sandwich he'd bought at the Colonial Deli and popped open the first of two beers. He was regretting not having taken a bag of Mattie's Virginia ham biscuits and pecan bars when he noticed a handwritten letter amid the stack of papers. The handwriting wasn't familiar, which piqued Tim's interest. Licking the Thousand Island sandwich dressing off his fingers, Tim carefully opened the letter. It was from Bud Burgess, head wine steward at the King's Arms Tavern. As a second-year law student, Bud was the only employee at the restaurant with more seniority than Tim. He said he knew Tim was away on "personal business," so he'd decided to write a note. Bud's fiancée had issued an ultimatum, demanding that they move in together to her apartment in Newport News and that Bud give up the small basement room in the house on Chandler Court, an approved off-campus facility, that he had rented for the past three years. He'd already moved out, and if Tim wanted the apartment, all he had to do was move his things in. Bud had talked to Mrs. Robson, owner of the rambling colonial house, who lived upstairs, and had told her that Tim was taking the apartment. She was pleased with the arrangement, just as long as the monthly rent of sixty-nine dollars was paid on time. Mrs. Robson trusted Bud's judgment, and in her opinion, any young man who worked at the King's Arms Tavern must be a trustworthy person. The key to the apartment was in the envelope. Tim sat back, astonished by this stroke of luck in what had otherwise been the worst week of his life.

It was Christmas time in Williamsburg. Every window in the historic district displayed an electric white candle that, as if by magic, was illuminated at five every evening and, by the same magic went dark after midnight. Decorations around doorways and windows were green with fresh pine and boxwood; nothing artificial was allowed. For added color, fresh fruits and vegetables might be carefully wired into the foliage: clusters of artichokes, oranges, apples, and pears often against a background of pecans and walnuts. Above the doorways of the most important homes, a fresh pineapple, the symbol of hospitality and welcoming, was ensconced within a choir of pinecones.

Tim bounded into the reception area of the King's Arms Tavern, still buttoning his white ruffled shirt as he prepared for the lunch crowd patiently waiting outside the front door on Duke of Gloucester Street. "I can't believe it," he said. Bud was filling the bar refrigerator with bottles of Liebfraumilch and Riesling, the two most popular and least expensive whites on the tavern's wine list.

"Brace yourself for a lot of fish and Lieb orders today," Bud said as he stacked the wine bottles in the cooler. "This holiday crowd looks really cheap." The less expensive items on the menu, such as the fish entree and the German wines, meant smaller tips for the waiters and subsequently an even smaller cut for Bud, who typically collected a percentage of the beverage check from each waiter.

"I mean the apartment on Chandler Court," Tim said. "Are you sure you want to move out?"

"I don't want to," Bud confided. "But Maryanne said she wouldn't spend another night in that 'flea-infested cave,' even though it's close to town. She's insisted I move into her apartment in Newport News. She came this week and packed up my clothes. So it's all yours, if you want it. I told Mrs. Robson you'd be moving in over the holidays."

"Sure, I guess." Tim still couldn't believe he would finally be able to move out of the dorm.

"You'll have to work out all the shit about giving up your room, but since it's midway through the year, no one will probably notice, until you're walking out of the Wren Building with your diploma. And at that point, who gives a shit?" Bud laughed.

"I can't tell you how much this means to me."

"I think the timing is probably good for you," Bud said before changing the subject. "Are you going to open the floodgates for lunch? You're on as host today, aren't you?"

"It's kind of like running the bulls at Pamplona," Tim joked as he opened the tavern door. "Welcome to the King's Arms Tavern," he said. "How many in your party today?"

It took Tim only two trips in the VW to transport all of his belongings from his room in Camm Dormitory to the small apartment on Chandler Court, a hidden cul-de-sac across campus off Jamestown Road. Mrs. Robson's house was a rambling Dutch Colonial built on the outskirts of the campus in the 1920s, in the era just before the Rockefeller Foundation poured millions of dollars into the community, rebuilding the colonial town of Williamsburg and establishing it as a national treasure.

The apartment, if you could call it that, was an enclosed cellar room with its own separate entrance beneath the porch of the house. The bathroom consisted of a shower stall with a plastic curtain, draining onto the floor. The kitchen area had one small sink; a bar-type refrigerator with little capacity and room for a single ice tray; and a hot plate placed on a cutting board on top of the refrigerator. The adjacent room had one single bed that also functioned as a sofa and a butterfly chair with a reading lamp. The unpolished hardwood floor was covered in a worn, braided oval carpet. The flat's door opened onto the street, and there were two small windows in the room looking out onto Mrs. Robson's garden, which was overgrown and in need of care.

Before unpacking his clothes and hanging them up on a rack in the kitchen, Tim found the electric candle lights he'd borrowed from the tavern's reserve supply and placed one in each window of his new home. Miraculously, there were electric outlets just below each window. The wiring of the room seemed designed for the traditional holiday ritual before any other practical consideration. Tim turned off the other lights in the small apartment, and in the glow of the two electric candles, he sprawled out on the lumpy bed and fell asleep.

Classes would let out for the Christmas holiday in one more week, and Tim had a lot of work to make up. He turned in his O'Neill paper, glad to be done with the morbid playwright obsessed with death. Tim's professors allowed him to make up two quizzes given in his absence. Now all he had to do was catch up on the reading he should have been doing for the past week. As an English major, Tim had elected to take four reading classes out of the five required courses he needed for the semester. He'd planned to work at the King's Arms Tavern over most of the holiday and use the downtime to study for finals in mid-January. He'd already decided not to go home to spend Christmas with his parents.

The pungent smell of wood-burning fires teased his nose as Tim walked down Duke of Gloucester Street on his way to the evening seating at the King's Arms. He passed Bruton Parish Church, glowing inside with the candlelight service about to begin. The town was quiet except for some tourists pouring out of Chownings Tavern, singing Christmas carols off-key after a long afternoon of drinking ale and dipping bread into Welsh rabbit. The electric candles in each window of the buildings in the historic district were now illuminated, creating a calm and secure postcard setting.

Tim kicked open the wooden gate leading to the outbuilding behind the tavern where the waiters and staff got dressed in their costumes for the evening performance called dinner. He stepped into the role every night, as though onstage. He wondered whether Red would approve of this performance. Tim stopped in front of his locker, his freshly ironed, white, ruffled "Tom Jones" shirt in hand, knowing that this act was about to close.

It turned out to be a good evening, with Tim handling three seatings in the Red Room, the prize location for high tippers. He had over fifty dollars in his pocket, a good take for any evening, when he walked up Duke of Gloucester Street toward Chandler Court, not even bothering to change out of his waiter costume. An occasional car headlight flashed him as he walked along the otherwise deserted historic street, a primitive ritual that passed for cruising in Williamsburg, which Tim found neither erotic nor amusing.

He approached the student center on Jamestown Road two blocks from his new apartment. The bulletin board was packed with familiar notes of students looking for rides, sales of used textbooks, or offers to join protest groups against the Vietnam War. The adjacent stand-alone phone kiosk was lonely and uninhabited.

Tim poured several quarters into the coin slot and punched in the numbers. "Hello, M ... is that you?"

"Tim? What a surprise," M said in his friendly southern accent. "I was hoping you'd call, but I never thought you actually would."

"Well, surprise. Here I am," Tim laughed. "What are you doing?"

"Waiting around for you to call," M teased.

"Where are you spending the Christmas holidays?" Tim asked, getting to the point.

"Well, I'm not going to Argentina. It's hot as hell there, and everyone goes to church and then stays at home with their families. And my friends tell me that the repression of students and anyone with long hair is still going on. Forget that! I'd rather be here in DC."

"How about coming to Williamsburg for a traditional American Christmas?" Tim suggested. "I have a new apartment. It's not much, but at least you'd have a place to stay—I mean, if you want to."

"Are you serious?" M asked.

The next day M arrived at the Greyhound bus station. Tim met him and showed his guest around the colonial town. It was Christmas in Williamsburg: no crass commercialism – no flocked trees or Santa Clauses slinging bells looking for contributions to the Salvation Army.

"You're very easy to get used to," M said as he woke up the next morning and brushed Tim's bangs out of his sleepy eyes.

"So are you," Tim said, turning over, not realizing until then that his guest was sleeping on the floor alongside the small bed. Tim's arm dangled like a broken limb off one side of the bed as he gently tugged at his friend's Jockey shorts.

M got up off the cold floor and crawled into the small cot next to Tim.

"You weren't kidding about this place being quaint," M joked, snuggling up to Tim as the two drifted off into a peaceful, warm sleep.

The little Christmas tree Tim had propped up in the middle of the room was a freebie he'd picked up from the supermarket on Richmond Road that was pulverizing unsold trees. It looked sad in the morning light. Its decorations were postcards from realtors hoping to list the Robson home for sale, a calendar from the local bank, a Snoopy Hallmark card from Tim's mother (the fifty-dollar check removed), and his sister's mundane card that looked like it might have come from the dealership where she'd bought her last car.

It was Christmas Day, and Tim had to be at work at eleven to set up for the busiest day of the year at the King's Arms. Tim had quietly slipped out of bed just after nine o'clock, pulling the blanket up over M, who was still asleep. He looked like an angel with his silky blond hair spread on the pillow. Tim had showered and shaved and had put a pot of water on the hot plate to make instant coffee. As he approached the bed, he could see M stirring.

"Merry Christmas," the blond angel said sleepily, as he loosened the towel Tim had wrapped around himself, letting it fall to the floor. Only the hissing of the boiling water on the hot plate forced Tim to extricate himself from the warm embrace of his Christmas angel.

"Christ, I'll have to take another shower after this," Tim laughed as he brought M a cup of coffee.

The King's Arms was fully booked, with a long waiting list of people hoping for a cancellation. There was a fixed menu, the only choice being turkey or ham for the main course, so service was quicker than usual, allowing the restaurant to cram in the maximum number of people throughout the day. By the time Tim served his last piece of pecan pie, around five in the afternoon, he had completed three full seatings. He had opted to work the first shift so that he could take M to the Williamsburg Inn for a formal Christmas dinner later that night.

"Here," Bud said, slipping Tim a bottle of Moet & Chandon champagne at the end of his shift. "You and your boyfriend have a good time tonight." The wine steward then winked as Tim prepared to leave the restaurant. "And tell Nat Merry Christmas for me. Sorry I couldn't make it by this year." Nat was the maître d' at the Williamsburg Inn. He had started as a bus boy over thirty years ago and had risen to the top position, controlling access to the coveted dining room. It was Nat who had guaranteed Tim that he would have a table for him and his guest on Christmas Day, despite reservations being closed for months.

The next few days, while Tim worked at the King's Arms, M explored the exhibition buildings of the restored area using Tim's student pass, which allowed access to any area of Colonial Williamsburg. M's favorite spot was the Governor's Palace garden, with its maze of boxwood hedges. He was a perfect guest, content to amuse himself while Tim worked long hours at the King's Arms. Evenings at the basement apartment on Chandler Court were romantic, with sandwiches from the Colonial Deli and bottles of cheap red wine. The electric candle lights glowed in the two windows of the apartment until the morning hours, as the two boys curled up nightly in the small bed, which they affectionately nicknamed "the manger."

Tim had worked out a schedule at the King's Arms that would allow him to have New Year's weekend off, since he'd promised Blade he'd spend the holiday in Georgetown. She was delighted when he told her he'd be bringing a guest: the young student from Argentina, whom she'd seen leaving through the back gate a few weeks earlier—the nice young man who had solved the mystery about a cold period in Spain.

CHAPTER 11

The drive on the interstate north from Williamsburg to Washington was uneventful, although holiday traffic was heavy. The old VW chugged along as faster cars and trucks whizzed by, exceeding the speed limit. Tim's hand drifted from the shifting knob between the two bucket seats to rest on M's knee, as his angel guest for the Christmas holiday dozed off in the passenger seat. The boys would spend New Year's at the Thirty-Third Street townhouse, with Blade doting over the beautiful blond student from Argentina.

Although the sex was great, and they had a lot of laughs together, Tim and M already understood that it was time for them to move on. And when M packed up his duffel bag to go back to his dorm on New Year's Day, it was a relief for both of them. Tim was relieved the holidays were over; now the reality of January and a new year was setting in.

Tim was glad to be back in his Chandler Court apartment cramming for finals. The holidays, his fling with M, and all the events surrounding Red's death already seemed a distant past. His work schedule at the

King's Arms was light since the first part of the year was traditionally a slow period, and the tavern was open only five days a week. His concentration on studying paid off when he took his final exams the last week of January. Tim received an A in the O'Neill course and B's in the others.

Tim had the application to Yale Drama School spread out on the small desk in his apartment. He knew it was pointless to apply for a deferment since the other students he knew who had done so had been turned down—all but those going on to med school. Despite his pessimism, Tim filled out the Yale application. Before sealing the envelope destined for New Haven, he reread the letter of recommendation Red had written for him. She'd sent it to him last fall when they'd first discussed his chances of getting into Yale Drama. The letter stated that she believed Tim had a promising career in the theatre, under the right direction, and that he was one of the most responsive and intuitive students she'd ever coached. Tim blushed at the high praise, and he thought of the one other letter Red had written on his behalf. It was when Tim was applying for an apprenticeship at St. Michael's Playhouse, an Equity-approved summer theatre in Winooski, Vermont. That was the summer between his freshman and sophomore years at William and Mary. The apprenticeship was more of a scholarship since it included room and board, plus an allowance of fifty dollars a week. Tim had convinced his parents it was a paying job, and since he'd demonstrated his willingness to help out with college expenses by working at the King's Arms Tavern, they'd agreed.

Although the summer theatre was operated by St. Michael's College in Burlington, it had an affiliation with Catholic University. One of the people Red knew was Father Frank Dolan, president of Catholic University. The priest had been a big fan of Red's since seeing her play Cleopatra at Olney: Red seemed to have a knack for attracting men of the cloth. The letter she'd written to Father Dolan was persuasive enough for Tim to be offered an apprenticeship without auditioning.

That summer, Tim was home in Westport only a week before his parents were driving him to Bridgeport airport. In the summertime,

Eastern Airlines operated a number of flights from small regional airports in Westchester and Fairfield Counties to resort areas around New England. There was one flight a day from Bridgeport to Burlington, Vermont, and it was decided that this was the easiest way for Tim to get to his summer job. Tim had saved enough money from working at the King's Arms to cover the cost of the air ticket. He was relieved that he did not have to spend hours in a car with his parents driving up Route 7 through the Berkshires to a small town in northern Vermont, a few miles from the Canadian border.

At the Burlington airport, Tim was met by John and Donna Rathburn, a young couple who were the technical director and production manager of St. Michael's Playhouse. They also shared directing responsibilities for some plays. The Rathburns were in the drama graduate program at Catholic University, and they hoped to pursue careers in regional theatre. They must have gotten some word from Father Dolan because they took Tim under their wing that summer, making sure he had an assignment in every production and an onstage part whenever appropriate.

That season at St. Michael's was relatively short, only six productions plus the showcase benefit put on by the apprentices at the end of the summer. The cast for all the shows was made up of the resident company of twelve Equity actors, who also covered as production crew whenever they were not onstage. A few of the lead parts were filled by visiting actors brought in for some specific role. Casting for all plays was completed during the two-week rehearsal period prior to the opening of the first production, so everyone, including the apprentices, knew what roles they would be playing during the season. Blocking for all the plays was done during those two weeks, and it was up to the actors to find time to learn their lines; once the season started, the company would be performing one play at night while rehearsing the next week's production during the day. For the apprentices, the schedule was particularly grueling: they had a two-hour class every morning starting at eight. Rehearsals for the entire company started at ten and went through to six or even later, breaking only for a short dinner in the St. Michael's College cafeteria before the evening curtain went up at eight thirty. There was no scheduled lunch break, but sandwiches, soft drinks, and apples were available in the cafeteria throughout the day. Another option, which most of the actors preferred, was a trip to the Frostie Stein, a food stand just a short walk from the playhouse. The Stein served Richardson's Root Beer in chilled beer mugs and proudly offered grinders, ten-inch hot dogs, onion rings, and an assortment of seafood. Tim was amazed at how good the food was at this little roadside stand, and he survived the summer on a diet of hot dogs, onion rings, and fish sticks.

When the final curtain of the evening performance came down, the actors and crew headed for the cocktail lounge at the Lincoln Inn, a five-minute drive up Highway 15 in Essex Junction. Recommended by Duncan Hines, the Lincoln Inn was the nicest place to stay without going into downtown Burlington. Many of the tourists who were guests there attended plays at St. Michael's, and they were thrilled to be in the lounge afterward with the lively young actors. Most nights, someone could be coaxed to play piano, and the actors would gather around and sing show tunes until last call, to the delight of everyone in the lounge. The manager of the motel welcomed the troupe of thespians because during July and August the cocktail lounge at the Lincoln Inn became *the* place to go late at night in the Burlington area. The rest of the year, the bar was deserted by nine o'clock.

John and Donna Rathburn made sure that Tim rode with them in their car to the lounge every night—along with a few of the other apprentices. A couple of the company actors had cars too, so there was transportation available for anyone who wanted to go to the local watering hole. Tim went every night because even after a long, exhausting day of classes, rehearsals, and set painting, he was too wound up to go to sleep. One luxury enjoyed by everyone in the company was a private room at the St. Michael's College dorm. Enrollment in summer school was light, so there was plenty of space to house the theatre crew. Tim would get back to his room a little after two in the morning, and for the next hour he'd study lines or write letters. That summer, he averaged about four hours of sleep per night, but he didn't care. He was having the time of his life.

The final production of the season was *Life with Father*, the popular play by Howard Lindsay and Russel Crouse that ran on Broadway for eight years and racked up over three thousand performances. Set in three acts, the play followed daily life in the household of Clarence Day, a wealthy Wall Street broker who lived in a handsome Victorian brownstone on Madison Avenue in the 1880s. Tim was cast as Whitney, the third of the four Day brothers. It was a stretch for him to play a preteen, but since he was the youngest-looking of all the male apprentices, he was the logical choice. Whitney's younger brother, Harlan, was played by a ten-year-old local boy from Essex Junction.

The very specific stage directions called for the Day family to be "redheaded in temperament, vital and spirited." Rather than deal with the inconvenience of fake-looking wigs, the actors playing the four Day sons agreed to dye their hair. Tim decided he would get a crew cut when he returned to Westport with the hope that traces of red would disappear before he arrived at William and Mary to begin his sophomore year.

The last week of the season was relaxed since the company was not rehearsing for another show the following week. The morning class for the apprentices was moved from eight to a more civilized start time of ten o'clock. Although the rest of the company had the days free, apprentices were busy rehearsing the benefit program, which was a scaled-back version of *The Wizard of Oz*, minus the singing and dancing. The familiar songs would be played on the piano as background music to the dialogue. This simple program was designed for children, with the goal of attracting a young audience who would experience live theatre for the first time. Running time for the show was just under an hour, with performances scheduled on the last Saturday of the season at 10:00 a.m. and 2:00 p.m. The ticket price of thirty-five cents was also an incentive to attract young people, and the shows traditionally sold out as soon as they were announced.

Tim's dyed red hair for his part in *Life with Father* proved to be an asset in his portrayal of the Tin Wood Man. He would point to his head when expressing fears of rust, before Dorothy came to his rescue with an oilcan. Performing before an audience of young children was a new experience for Tim and the other apprentices. The children talked to the actors throughout the performance; some even cried when the Wicked Witch came onstage. It was an exercise in control for the actors, a daunting challenge to stay in character, with chaos possible throughout the audience.

That last Saturday of the season was an exhausting day for the apprentices: two performances of *The Wizard of Oz* during the day followed by *Life with Father* at night. During that week when the apprentices finished rehearsals around four in the afternoon, Tim would borrow John Rathburn's bicycle and ride out to the state beach on Lake Champlain. There he stretched out on the pebbly shore and watched cotton-candy clouds float across the blue New England sky. He thought about how lucky he was to have Red as a mentor. How could he ever repay her for all she'd done for him, and all the encouragement she constantly supplied, when his own family was so negative. Reflective moments such as these inevitably led to thoughts of Jeffrey, and as Tim splashed his face with cold water from the lake, he looked at his reflection in the clear shallow water and wondered whether his twin brother would have looked just like him. Tim became enamored of that wavy reflection, determined to find out what had happened to Jeffrey.

The final performance that season was a Sunday matinee of *Life with Father*, a fundraiser to help reduce the deficit, inevitably run up every year. All tickets were ten dollars, but each member of the company was allotted two free tickets. Tim invited his parents, but Blade announced that she'd intended to come as well. Tim's dad and sister conveniently bowed out, happy not to have to endure a long ride to Vermont. It was agreed that Tim's mother, Barbara, and Blade would go and that Tim would ride back to Westport with them once he'd wrapped up his apprentice duties at St. Michael's.

A week earlier, Tim had received a postcard from Red saying she'd been invited by Father Dolan to come to the closing performance. The priest had offered to pick her up early Sunday morning to arrive in time for the matinee and then drive back to Connecticut after the cast party. It would be a long day, but it was the only way Red could possibly attend, since she was taping *Another World* on Monday. Father Dolan had to be in New York City that day for a meeting with Cardinal Spellman, so it worked out well for both of them. Father Dolan would also enjoy the company of the charming actress during the long ride up through New England, and most likely he would try to convince Red to return to Olney in some plum role the following season, provided the producers of the soap opera were willing to write her out for two months.

One of the perks Father Dolan enjoyed as president of Catholic University was a chauffeur-driven Cadillac at his disposal. It was a privilege he took full advantage of, and he had even managed to get a special vanity Maryland license plate that read "8:30"—the traditional theatre evening curtain time.

Tim made reservations for his mom and aunt to stay at the Lincoln Inn, and the plan was that they would arrive late Saturday afternoon and meet Tim for an early dinner before his evening performance. They would not arrive in time to see *The Wizard of Oz*. All went as planned, and the ladies went to bed early that night, leaving Tim to hang out with his friends in the Lincoln Inn cocktail lounge as usual for one last night of show tunes and drinking.

The next morning, after breakfast, Tim gave Blade and his mom a tour of the theatre, taking them backstage to show them the elaborate Victorian set and the extensive props and costumes. Tim's mom still hadn't gotten over the shock of her son's red hair, though Blade thought it was charming. Tim introduced his guests to John and Donna Rathburn, who were effusive in their praise of Tim's hard work that summer. There was time for a stop at the Frosty Stein before Tim had to report for a last round of notes before the final matinee.

"Root beer in a chilled mug," Blade gushed. "I haven't had that since I was a little girl."

"I lived on root beer, hot dogs, and fish sticks all summer," Tim laughed, glad that his mom and aunt were there to see him onstage. "I'd better get going. Your tickets are at the box office in my name. I'll see you afterward at the wrap party. They're setting up a buffet in the lobby and a full bar on the stage."

"Sounds very festive," Blade said.

"I'm sure it will be nice," Tim assured her.

"Good luck," Tim's mom said. She then quickly put her hand to her mouth. "Oh, dear! I don't think I'm supposed to say that."

"It's okay, Mom. Just a superstition," Tim said, kissing her on the cheek.

As he walked across the lawn to the theatre, Tim saw the pale blue Cadillac with the famous license plate pull into the parking lot. He wished he could run over and say hello to Red, but he didn't want to be late for the last set of notes. He would have to wait until after the show to see his mentor.

The final performance ran longer than usual, with the play interrupted by extended laughter and bursts of applause from an enthusiastic, friendly audience. The cast received a standing ovation when the entire company assembled onstage for the final curtain call. Tim quickly changed out of costume and washed off his stage makeup. There was nothing he could do about the red hair.

The party was well underway by the time Tim made his way to the lobby. He could see Red talking to Blade and his mom in front of the box office, where the actress was flanked by fans asking for her autograph. She saw Tim trying to make his way through the crowd and immediately broke away from a group of teenage girls holding copies of *Soap Opera Digest* with her picture on the cover.

"Tim," Red said, wrapping her arms around him. "You were wonderful."

"Thank you," he said, blushing from the compliment. "I'm really glad you could make it."

Arm in arm, the two wedged their way back across the lobby to join Tim's mom and Blade.

"Barbara, your son is a very talented young man," Red pointed out.

"Yes. But I'm glad he's getting his education so he can make a living someday."

"Actors need to know how to read too," Red commented dryly.

Tim extricated himself from the conversation by offering to get drinks for the women. He detected coolness between his mom and Red. The two had met only once and briefly after his workshop performance in *Our Town* at the White Barn Theatre. He was glad Blade was there to act as a buffer. When he returned with glasses of wine, Red was gone, having been pulled away by Father Dolan, who wanted to introduce her to some wealthy patrons of St. Michael's Playhouse.

"Red said that with your dyed hair you could pass for her son," Blade laughed, not noticing how her comment made Barbara wince.

"It's hideous," Tim's mom said tersely. "I hope you're getting it cut once you get home."

"Don't worry; I'm having it shaved off." Then, changing the subject, Tim suggested, "How about some food? The buffet looks really good."

The three got in line, plates in hand, and then moved into the theatre where they sat in the orchestra to eat their dinner of sliced roast beef and potato salad. Tim could see Father Dolan and Red were engaged in conversation with John and Donna Rathburn in the crowded lobby.

"That young Tim is quite exceptional," Father Dolan confided to the others. "I couldn't take my eyes off him when he was onstage. He has quite a presence."

"Yes," Red agreed, looking over at Tim across the theatre. "And that's not something you can teach. It's a gift."

"He reminds me of a young Olivier," the priest offered.

"Yes, of course he's handsome, but given the right training, he could have a career in theatre." Red predicted.

"Do you think we could get him to consider the graduate program at Catholic U?" Father Dolan asked.

"He's talking about Yale, but either program would be good for him," Red suggested.

"We'd better get going," Father Dolan suddenly said, looking at his watch. "Sunday traffic on Route 7 is going to be slow." Turning to John and Donna Rathburn, he said, "See you back on campus in a few weeks. And congratulations on a fine season here at St. Michael's."

The actress and the priest worked their way through the throng of theatergoers in the lobby to say good-bye to Tim, Barbara, and Blade.

"Sorry we have to run," Red apologized, wrapping her arm around Tim and kissing him on the cheek. "But it's a long drive back to Westport, and I have to work tomorrow."

"Thanks for coming," Tim said. "It really meant a lot to me."

"Would not have missed it! And you're wonderful as a redhead," she laughed. "Tim … you should come by next Sunday. I'm having some of the kids up from the show for brunch. It's the start of our two-week summer hiatus."

"I'd love to, if I won't be intruding."

"Nonsense! You know you're welcome," the actress said.

"I hope Tim isn't becoming a pest," Barbara interjected.

"Not at all. He's my brightest student." Turning to Tim, she added, "Besides, Nick Agropolis, the dean of Yale Drama, is coming. I'd like you to meet him."

Tim's mom frowned at the suggestion, but she said nothing.

"Thanks again for coming. I'll see you Sunday," Tim said as the actress and the priest left the theatre to get into the waiting Cadillac with the "8:30" license plate. The chauffeur eased the car through the gates of St. Michael's and onto the highway for the long, scenic drive through the Berkshires on the way to Westport.

"You know, Frank," the actress said, breaking a long silence, "I don't think Tim's parents are very supportive of his acting ambitions. I haven't met the father, but if Barbara is any indication, I think the boy has a rough battle ahead."

"Pity," the priest mused, gazing out the car window at the leafy Vermont countryside. "A young Olivier!"

CHAPTER 12

Tim looked over the application to Yale Drama School, making sure he had filled in all the required fields. He reread the letter of recommendation from Red once more and blushed at her effusive praise. He'd told her that he was concerned about the draft and that it was hopeless for a drama major to expect a deferment. She'd dismissed the subject, advising Tim not to worry about things over which he had no control, to move ahead with his life, and to face issues if and when they arose. Red had a remarkable talent for ignoring reality, a trait that perhaps contributed to her considerable success as an actress. Tim had qualms about sending a letter of recommendation from a dead person, but he knew Red would be furious if he didn't take advantage of her influence, even posthumously. He'd not been back to Arlington Cemetery since he'd left the narcissus on her grave two days after the burial. While in Georgetown over the New Year's holiday, he easily could have made the trip across the Potomac, but he hadn't.

Tim slipped the letter addressed to Nick Agropolis into a yellow manila envelope along with the application forms. Before sealing the glued flap and fastening the metal clip, he took a ballpoint pen and carefully etched the eerie Kilroy ghost figure with the familiar words "Jeffrey Was Here" on the lip of the envelope that was covered by the flap. It was after five o'clock, so he would have to wait until tomorrow to take the application to the post office for mailing.

Although it was late, Tim decided to drop by Harold Spivey's office to discuss his report date for *The Common Glory* rehearsals. Spivey's office was in Phi Beta Kappa Hall, a short distance from Tim's Chandler Court apartment. Tim walked down Jamestown Road, crossed Barksdale Athletic Field, and entered the theatre building through the stage door. The corridor was lined with black-and-white photos of past productions, and Tim paused to study the one from *Our Town* where George and Emily were perched on ladders talking to each other, as though from their bedroom windows. It was the role Tim was most proud of, in large part due to Red's coaching in the workshop production.

Spivey was in his office reading a script, a coffee mug with a shot of Jack Daniels sitting discreetly within arm's reach on the cluttered desk.

"Tim, what a nice surprise. Come in."

"Thanks. I hope I'm not interrupting."

"Not at all. You know I always have time for you," Spivey said.

"I wanted to talk to you about *The Common Glory*." Tim repeated what he had written in a note to the professor before the holidays: he wanted to be in the outdoor pageant again, but his aunt was taking him to South America as a graduation present, and he would have to report late for rehearsals.

"Can you be here on Monday the nineteenth?" the director asked, looking at his calendar.

"Yes, that will work out. We get back the Saturday before."

"Okay. You know the blocking, and the cues are the same as last year. I'll just work around you the first week. That'll still give you a full week for tech and dress rehearsals. We open on the twenty-sixth."

"I really appreciate this," Tim said.

"And"—the director paused dramatically—"no crazy pranks this year." He was referring to the incident last summer when someone replaced the pencil sketch of Patty Jefferson with a photo of a gorilla wearing a blond wig. The picture frame prop was used every night in a scene where Thomas Jefferson reflects on his daughter, whom he hasn't seen for several months. He picks up the framed picture and, gazing at her sweet image, longs for the day when he will see her again. The night of the prank, however, the actor playing Jefferson burst into uncontrollable laughter when he saw the photo of the primate in the blond wig, dropping the prop on the cement stage floor, where it shattered into pieces. It was toward the end of the season, and the actors were becoming bored with performing in the same corny outdoor drama every night.

Spivey, who played the narrator of the pageant, witnessed this unprofessional breach of discipline, and after the performance, he immediately called a meeting of the entire company. He demanded to know who was responsible for the incident, but no one came forward. And even though most of the actors knew who the culprits were—it would have taken the cooperation of more than one to pull off such a stunt—the entire company remained silent. Furious and determined not to have a repeat incident, Spivey docked everybody one night's pay. Although there was grumbling, especially among the stage crew, the general consensus was that the joke had been worth it to break the monotony of the season. The incident was raucously rehashed at parties the rest of the summer.

"You've got to admit it was funny," Tim chuckled.

"I do not," Spivey said, still miffed. "It was downright unprofessional."

"Well, no more crazy pranks this season," Tim conceded.

Last year had been Tim's first season in *The Common Glory*. He'd been cast primarily as a dancer, but he'd also had nonspeaking roles in the many crowd scenes. That meant being onstage almost the entire night, with numerous costume changes. Performing in an amphitheatre was a new experience for Tim. First there was the DDT. Every night at seven o'clock the fumigation truck would roll down the dirt road to the outdoor theatre and spray a mist of poison across the stage, the bleachers, and the surrounding woods. The actors were cautioned to avoid that immediate area for fifteen minutes, until the noxious fumes dissipated. But on numerous hot, muggy nights, the clouds of eye-stinging gas still loomed ominously. Although the practice might have been somewhat effective in reducing the infestation of pesky mosquitoes that bred profusely on the shores of Lake Matoaka, the show's producers gave little thought to the potential harm this nightly practice might be doing to the lungs of the cast and crew.

The DDT sprayings did nothing to deter the frogs and water moccasins that inevitably found their way onto the stage, to the dismay of the performers. For the most part the creatures were harmless and easily frightened off by the commotion around them, but the reptiles posed an unwanted distraction to the actors.

Then there was the hardship of having to dance on a concrete stage. Shin splints were common; ACE bandages and painkillers became a way of life for the dancers that summer.

Tim did not have his own apartment that summer before his senior year, so he was housed along with the rest of the company in the Ludwell complex, about a mile from the amphitheatre. The Ludwell apartments had originally been built as military housing during World War II, but in recent years the college had taken over the complex and used it as overflow housing, mostly for female students, while a new dorm was being built. Bus service was provided for the long trek back and forth to campus, but students who ended up at Ludwell groused that they were marooned and cut off from daily campus activities. The college, however, was delighted when the producers of *The Common Glory* took over the facility for the summer months.

Most of the units were two-bedroom apartments with a small kitchenette and a living/dining room area. Each apartment could accommodate four actors, two in each bedroom. The few married couples in the company had the luxury of an apartment to themselves, and the extra bedroom often provided a place to stay for visiting guests. Some of the actors, including Tim, had cars, so at seven every night, a caravan would form for the short drive to the amphitheatre. After the performance, there would be a mad dash to the Colonial Deli on Richmond Road for last call. The rowdy actors would stock up on beer, pizza, and meatball grinders before returning to Ludwell for a night of partying.

Saturday nights were different. Management hosted a weekly barbecue for the cast, crew, and guests after the final performance of the week. Sundays were dark, so everyone could party until the sun came up, not having to worry about a performance the next day. The weekly bash was usually held at a picnic area in the woods behind the theatre, far from any local Williamsburg residents. It was at one of these weekly parties early in the summer that Tim met Dan Daniels, a guest of Mimi Hutchens, the costume mistress for *The Common Glory*. Like most of the production crew, Mimi was a local. She and Dan had attended Hampton High School together and had dated for a while. He'd taken her to the senior prom. Their dating then grew into a platonic friendship when Dan confided to Mimi that he thought he was gay. Mimi, who was barely five feet tall and considerably overweight, accepted the fact that she was unlikely to have a real boyfriend anytime soon, so she settled for going out with Dan on convenience dates. They enjoyed each other's company, and Dan was a bit starstruck at hanging out with the zany theatre people Mimi worked with.

After graduating Hampton High, Dan enrolled in a trade school where he studied to become a draftsman. He knew he would never go to college. His grades were poor, and there was no way his mom could afford state school tuition even if he managed to get accepted. Dan lived with his mom at the Lord Paget trailer park in Hampton Roads. She had a job as a hairdresser at Miss Selana's beauty parlor, and Dan worked after school as a cashier at the 7-Eleven. Together they were able to make ends meet. Shortly before Dan was born, his father, an ensign in the navy, had shipped out on an aircraft carrier deployed somewhere in the Mediterranean. He'd never returned, as promised, to marry Loretta, Dan's mom.

Upon completion of his draftsman course, Dan was hired by the Newport News Shipbuilding and Dry Dock Company, where he spent hours meticulously drawing blueprints for nuclear-powered submarines. He was particularly adept at this detailed and monotonous task, and he was soon granted the needed low-level security clearance, since he was working on sensitive military documents. Dan was terrified that if his supervisor discovered he was gay, he would be fired. He was extremely circumspect and never went to the gay bars in Norfolk, choosing instead to make the three-hour drive to DC if he wanted to be in the company of other gay men.

Dan's job at the shipyard paid well, and with overtime on Saturday mornings, he was able to buy a car. He no longer had to suffer the humiliation of driving Loretta's rusted Ford Falcon. Instead he bought a 1963 Corvette Stingray Convertible from one of the engineers at the shipyard who was getting married. The classic car was in excellent shape, painted fawn beige with a black canvas top. Every Saturday when he got off work, Dan washed the car and applied a light coat of wax, whether it was needed or not. He wiped Armor-All on the tires with a damp cloth and cleaned the polished chrome spinner wheels with warm soapy water. The sports car looked as though it had just been driven off the showroom floor.

Dan was equally fastidious in how he dressed. Every day, he wore a freshly starched shirt that he had ironed and placed on a hanger before going to bed the previous night. He wouldn't consider wearing a shirt more than once before washing it. His khaki slacks were always pressed with a sharp crease, and his brown penny loafers were buffed to a perfect shine. He looked like he was heading for a military inspection every morning when he passed through the security gates of the Newport News Shipbuilding and Dry Dock Company.

Tim noticed Dan when Mimi first brought him to the Saturday night cast party as her guest. Dan was a striking figure among the scruffy actors and stagehands. He took the same care with his casual clothes as he did when dressing for work at the shipyard. His Bermuda shorts were pressed, and the pale blue polo shirt he was wearing fit his well-formed body snugly, without a wrinkle. His honey-colored hair was cropped short around the neck and ears, leaving a soft wave he combed back from his tanned forehead. Mimi liked to describe her handsome escort as "Ashley" from *Gone with the Wind*, and being a native Virginian, Dan had a slight southern accent to complete the portrait.

Looking at Mimi and Dan, Tim quickly surmised they were just friends, so he didn't hesitate to approach Dan to start up a conversation. Dan was immediately taken by the young actor, and their casual conversation quickly turned into a flirtatious exchange. Mimi picked up on what was happening and, though disappointed, graciously excused herself, telling Dan that she was tired and getting a ride home with her sister Ruthie, who also worked in the costume department.

"Do you need a lift?" Dan asked Tim as the two sat on a picnic table drinking beer. They'd wandered away from the rest of the partying crowd, which was now singing show tunes and doing celebrity impersonations around the fire in the barbecue pit.

"That'd be great, if you don't mind," Tim said.

"No problem." Dan put his beer down on the wooden picnic table and placed a hand on Tim's knee.

"I live at Ludwell off Jamestown Road," Tim explained, resting his palm on top of Dan's hand, and pressing gently.

"I know where that is," Dan said. "Let's go. I'm parked down the road."

"Just a minute," Tim said, getting up. "I need to talk to Jimmy first."

Jimmy Stiles was the dance captain and Tim's roommate at Ludwell. Slipping him the keys to the Volkswagen, Tim asked, "Would you mind driving my car back to Ludwell? I'm getting a ride with Dan."

"Sure, kid," Jimmy smirked. "Have fun with 'Ashley.'"

Dan and Tim walked hand in hand along the wooded path of the dirt-road entrance to the amphitheatre. Tim tried to hide his amazement when Dan opened the passenger door of the gleaming tan sports car.

"It's my new toy," Dan said, smiling.

"Wow!" Tim was impressed. "I feel like Cinderella."

Tim was grateful that Jimmy had agreed to take care of his car. Tim shared an apartment with Jimmy and two other dancers. He and Jimmy Stiles had one bedroom; two other male dancers slept in the second one. Tim was astounded when he found out that Jimmy Stiles was from Elkton, Maryland, and that he knew JoEllen Taylor. The two had taken ballet classes at the Arianna Foote Academy of Dance when they were in high school. When Jimmy found out Tim knew JoEllen, he became a bit cool and somewhat distant. He wasn't happy that someone in the company, much less his roommate, knew of his humble background growing up in rural Maryland.

Tim assumed that Jimmy was gay, although the two had never discussed the issue. When they'd first met, Tim thought Jimmy was extremely attractive. He had a great body and an effervescent personality. Although the two shared a bedroom that summer, there was never physical contact. Jimmy went out of his way not to socialize with any openly gay members of the company. His constant companion was Gwyneth Dawn, a young dancer who'd studied with the Ballet Russe. She was the quintessential flower child of the company, beautiful and delicate as a butterfly. Everyone assumed that Gwyneth Dawn was not her real name, but no one questioned her. Ultimately, Gwen would go on to win a Golden Globe and get an Oscar nomination for best supporting actress for a role she created in a Mel Brooks film, but that summer in Williamsburg she was focused on having sex with every man in the company, straight or gay.

"It's not much," Tim apologized as he led Dan up the outside stairway to his second-floor apartment at Ludwell.

"Nicer than where I live," Dan said without elaborating about the fold-out cot he slept on in his mom's trailer.

"Beer?"

"No, thanks. Come here." Dan slid outstretched onto the sofa in the living area. Tim kneeled into Dan's open arms, and the two seemed to melt together, kissing passionately as Dan slid a hand along Tim's thigh.

"Wait," Tim said, suddenly withdrawing, pressing his hand on the firm bulge in Dan's perfectly pressed Bermuda shorts. "My roommates will be coming back, and I don't want us to be caught with our pants down when they come in."

"They probably wouldn't mind," Dan said with a grin.

"No, but I would," Tim said, getting up.

"Thanks," Dan said, looking Tim directly in the eyes. "You're nice."

"I try." Tim tapped Dan gently on the cheek.

Dan and Tim became what could be called an item for the rest of the summer. Tim made an arrangement with Jimmy Stiles that gave him use of the bedroom on Saturday nights whenever Dan stayed over, after the weekly cast party. Dan was popular with the cast and crew, who followed Mimi Hutchens's lead in affectionately calling him "Ashley." Mimi was pleased to assume the role of Dolly Levi—the matchmaker behind the pairing of the two handsome young men.

The shining tan Corvette was parked outside the Ludlow apartments every Saturday night. On Sundays, Dan and Tim would drive to Virginia Beach, crossing through the Chesapeake Bay Bridge tunnel in the Corvette with the top down. They spent the days splashing in the surf, spreading out on beach towels in the sand dunes, playfully dripping baby oil on each other's backs. Late in the afternoon, they'd rinse off in the public shower and then take turns changing into clean shorts and T-shirts behind the low open door of the Corvette.

Sunday nights became a tradition with dinner at Nick's Seafood Pavilion in Yorktown. Nick's was a family-owned Greek restaurant nestled under the York River bridge that linked Yorktown to Gloucester Point. Dan and Tim split the check every week because Nick's was pricier than most of the local restaurants catering to Williamsburg college students. The two often splurged and ordered the special lobster salad. After dinner, the boys would walk across the street to the Wharf, a local pub owned by a gay man from one of the most prominent families in Yorktown. The Wharf was a converted old boathouse, sitting right out on the wooden dock along the river. There was a piano inside, and on Sunday nights, when the cast from *The Common Glory* descended, the pub became a riot of actors singing obscure show tunes. The Wharf was the closest thing to a gay bar in the area outside Norfolk, especially whenever single guys from the Coast Guard station wandered in. On those nights, there was a definite undertone of cruising in the bar even though the crowd was mixed. At first Dan was nervous about going to the Wharf, but Tim enjoyed it, and any bar filled with a crowd of boisterous theatre people was bound to foster a liberal atmosphere.

One night when Dan and Tim were heading to the bar after dinner at Nick's, they saw Gwen and Jimmy Stiles arguing in the Wharf parking lot.

"Fine," Jimmy said, slamming the door of the Volkswagen and driving off in a cloud of sand and pebbles. Tim had let Jimmy Stiles use his car on weekends whenever he was riding around with Dan in the Corvette. It was small payback for Jimmy sleeping on the sofa Saturday nights whenever Dan stayed over in the Ludwell apartment.

"What was that all about?" Tim asked.

"Oh, nothing. Just stupid," Gwen said, exasperated. Switching to her usual sweet, little girl voice, Gwen asked, "Do you think I could get a ride back with you guys later?"

"Well, it'll be a little tight, but I guess you could sit on Tim's lap," Dan offered.

"That could be fun," Gwen flirted.

The trio went into the Wharf and stayed for two beers before Dan looked at his watch and suggested they head back to Williamsburg. Dan did not sleep over at the Ludwell apartment on Sunday nights because he had to report for work in the shipyard at seven thirty the next morning. On Sundays, Dan would drop Tim off after a day at the beach and dinner at Nick's and then drive back to the Lord Paget motor court to sleep on the rollaway bed in Loretta's trailer. As the summer wore on, Tim became increasingly frustrated with the limitations of his relationship with Dan. He looked forward to starting his senior-year classes and having a more active social life, with an occasional weekend trip to Georgetown.

That night, the three piled into the Corvette, with Gwen sitting on Tim's lap. It was a sticky, humid night as the sports car edged onto Colonial Parkway for the trip back to Williamsburg. The scent of magnolia and jasmine blossoms hung like heavy perfume in the night air while the chickadees and bullfrogs competed in a cacophony of sounds. Tim was starting to get a cramp in his left thigh where Gwen was perched when she chirped cheerfully, "Let's all go for a swim."

"What? Now?" Dan asked.

"Sure. The state beach is just up the road, about a mile. Come on. It'll be fun. Besides, it's hot as hell, and I'm all sticky," Gwen argued.

"Tim?" Dan said, deferring to his friend.

"I'm game if everybody else is," he said, thinking it would be a relief to get out of the cramped sports car.

Dan eased the Corvette off the parkway and down the gravel road into the state beach parking lot. Signs were posted warning that the beach closed at sunset, so there was no one there.

"We're not supposed to be here," Dan cautioned as he turned off the ignition.

"What are they going to do? Arrest us?" Gwen quipped.

"Tim, our trunks are in the gym bag behind your seat," Dan said.

"Oh no," Gwen objected. "I'm not going to be the only one without a suit."

Dan shot a look at Tim, who was grinning.

"You guys aren't bashful, are you?" Gwen teased, peeling off her tank top to reveal two small, firm breasts. She looked like a little boy as she inched her cut-off Levi shorts down around her ankles. The dimples on her cream-pie face were mirrored on the top of her melon-shaped butt, and a small powder puff of white curls below her navel was the only hair on her body. Gwen reminded Tim of the shepherd boy statue in the Christmas manger erected every year at Assumption Church.

Tim was relaxed enough from the beers at the Wharf to just shrug his shoulders at Dan, and then, as if in submission, he slipped out of his shorts and T-shirt. Dan immediately followed, and the trio left a small pile of clothes by the shore as they splashed giddily into the warm water of the York River. The three were shrieking and laughing, taking turns dunking each other and playing crocodile, when their revelry was abruptly interrupted by a blinding spotlight and a stern voice on a bullhorn demanding they get out of the water—now. The flashing light on top of the state trooper's patrol car illuminated the shoreline where the three swimmers scrambled for their clothes. The officer, in his Smokey Bear hat, looked more amused than gruff when he reprimanded them, saying that if he caught them again, he would issue a citation for trespassing.

The three hastily put on their clothes and piled back into the Corvette, as the policeman watched with arms folded. Dan started the engine of the sports car and carefully drove out of the parking lot and back onto Colonial Parkway. Gwen turned and blew a kiss to the state trooper as the three headed back to Williamsburg.

Now, in Professor Spivey's office in the spring semester of his senior year, Tim was relieved that he'd initiated the conversation about his reporting date for *The Common Glory* rehearsals. Although it was on his mind, Tim decided not to mention the possibility of his being drafted. Instead, he followed Red's advice to not pour energy into things over which he had no control. Just as Tim was turning to leave his office, Professor Spivey took a sip of Jack Daniels from the coffee mug and announced, "I'm directing *Under Milk Wood* this spring, and I'd like you to audition. It's my favorite Dylan Thomas play, more like a long poem, and there are some goods parts for you—particularly one of the drowned."

"Sounds perfect," Tim laughed, "seeing I'm way over my head this semester."

Tim had four reading classes he still needed to complete for his degree in English. But somehow he'd work in the Dylan Thomas play for Professor Spivey and also find time for his job at the King's Arms Tavern. Aside from a break during the Presidents' Day holiday, when he went to DC for a sex-filled fling with M, and a visit with Blade, Tim's social life was nonexistent for the next couple of months. In late March, when he was cramming for midterms, he took a break one day to check his post office box, which he hadn't opened in over a week. It was packed with two issues of *Time* magazine, the usual junk mail, an allowance check from his mom, and a letter from Yale.

"Blade," Tim said breathlessly into the phone a few minutes later. "It's from Nick Agropolis."

"Yes, Tim. I know who he is," Blade replied patiently, although she knew what was coming.

"I've been accepted at Yale Drama School."

"Of course you have, dear. Is that a surprise?"

"A surprise?" Tim said incredulously. "What am I going to do?"

"You're going to New Haven in September," Blade said matter-of-factly.

"But how?" Tim tried to come down off the euphoria of the moment. "Do you know what the tuition is?"

"Actually, I do," Blade said, becoming serious. "I've discussed this with Father Dolan, who of course wants you to go to Catholic U."

"I didn't even apply," Tim said dismissively.

"I know. It was Yale or nothing."

"You know what they say about being careful what you wish for. Now what am I going to do? Mom and Dad made it very clear that they wouldn't pay."

"Have you told them yet?" Blade probed.

"No. You're the only one who knows. Besides, what are they going to do? Wish me good luck?"

"They might feel differently knowing you're actually accepted," Blade said without conviction.

"I'm not even going there," Tim said disgustedly.

"Fortunately, you don't have to ask them."

"I don't?"

"No! I'm going to pay your tuition," Blade said decisively.

Tim was astounded by his aunt's suggestion. "Do you know what it costs?"

"Yes, I know exactly what it costs. You're going. End of discussion."

Tim knew it was pointless to argue with his aunt, and he was secretly overjoyed at her generous offer. Their conversation turned to the more immediate matter of Tim's graduation from William and Mary in three weeks. Each senior was entitled to four tickets for the ceremony. It had long been understood that Tim's parents, his sister Kathy, and his aunt Blade would attend. In her typical well-organized way, Blade had booked rooms at the Williamsburg Inn as soon as the graduation date was announced. Commencement would take place on the first Friday in June; Blade and Tim would leave for their South American adventure the following Sunday.

Tim's graduating class included just over five hundred students, a record number for the venerable institution founded in 1693. The program was scheduled to begin at ten in the morning, and by the time the seniors marched in cap and gown into the front rows of folding chairs, the temperature was well into the eighties. It was a sweltering, humid day, with no breeze. Because of the size of the class and the number of guests, the event had to be held outdoors on the sprawling lawn in front of the Wren Building. There was no indoor facility on the campus large enough to accommodate such a crowd.

It was after one o' clock before the last diploma had been handed out and the speakers had finished their inspirational words. The graduating class threw their caps into the air with a loud cheer, and polite, if relieved, applause arose from the audience that had been suffering in the oppressive heat for over three hours.

Tim found his way through the crowd to his family, who were waiting patiently under the shade of a magnolia tree in front of the president's house. Blade was fanning herself with a large spade-shaped bamboo hand fan, and Tim's dad was wiping sweat from his forehead with a white handkerchief. Kathy was sitting on the brick steps of the president's house, looking bored.

"Well, that was something," Barbara said, kissing her son lightly on the cheek.

"Congratulations, son," Tim's dad added. "You really made it."

"Oh, Tim. We're all so proud of you," Blade gushed as she fluttered around her nephew like a butterfly, waving the bamboo fan in the air.

"Come on back to the apartment," Tim said. "I've got cold drinks and something to eat. We can cool off and relax. Sorry about this heat, but that's summer in Williamsburg."

Tim led his family along the brick sidewalk on Jamestown Road to the small Chandler Court apartment where Bud Burgess, the wine steward from the King's Arms, was waiting. Bud had set up a full bar, including glasses and setups to make Bottoms Up cocktails. Tim had ordered a cheese tray, potato salad, and finger sandwiches from the Colonial Deli so that they would have something to nibble on with their cocktails.

"This should tide us over until dinner," Tim said, toasting his guests. "We have a reservation tonight at the King's Arms at seven."

"You're in the Red Room," Bud announced. "And I'll be waiting on you."

"Now that's service," Tim beamed, pleased to be surrounded by his family on this milestone day in his life. Bud had set up aluminum folding chairs on the lawn outside the apartment facing Mrs. Robson's rose garden, where the group spent the rest of the afternoon.

"I think we should be getting back to the hotel," Barbara announced, getting up. "I want to shower and freshen up before dinner."

"How's the Inn?" Tim asked.

"Fine," his sister Kathy said, "if you don't mind not having a TV in the room."

"People don't usually come to Williamsburg to watch television," Tim shot back defensively.

"Sorry, I forgot for a minute that we're in the Dark Ages," Kathy said. "I guess I should be thankful we have lights and running water."

Dinner at the King's Arms turned into a special occasion, with Bud waiting on Tim's family and other waiters coming by during the course of the meal. Several congratulated Tim and wished him the best at Yale Drama School in the fall. Tim's parents remained cool to the idea of their son going to Yale to get a degree in theatre arts, but they couldn't object too strenuously since they were not paying for it. Blade's offer to underwrite her nephew's graduate school expenses had created tension with Tim's parents, but she dealt with it as she did other unpleasant issues: she chose to ignore it and move ahead with her life.

It was a balmy evening as the group strolled up Duke of Gloucester Street after dinner. "I'm going to miss Williamsburg," Tim said wistfully. "It's been a great four years."

"Well, at least with a degree in English, you can always teach," Tim's dad offered. Tim winced at his father's practical suggestion. "It's always good to have a fallback position—an option," his dad continued.

"Sure, Dad. I can always teach," Tim said with a shrug, feeling the joy of the day evaporating like air from a pricked balloon.

Tim's dad pulled up to the Chandler Court apartment in his Lincoln at nine the next morning as agreed. The family had checked out of the Williamsburg Inn and was ready for the three-hour drive to Washington, DC. The plan was to drop Blade and Tim off in Georgetown. Tim's mom, dad, and sister would then continue on to Westport. The first leg of the trip would be cramped, with five adults and their luggage stuffed into the car. Tim straddled the backseat, wedged between his sister and his mom, while Blade rode shotgun in the front seat next to Tim's dad. It could have been a scene out of *The Beverly Hillbillies*.

"Well, that went pretty well," Blade laughed later on, as she toasted Tim with a tumbler of Jim Beam. She and Tim had settled into the drawing room at Thirty-Third Street as the others continued the drive on to Westport.

"Anything less than a fistfight can be considered a win, I guess," Tim said good-naturedly.

"They mean well," Blade conceded. "They just don't understand you."

"And you do?" Tim challenged, emboldened by the Dewar's he was drinking.

"More than you know, dear. More than you know."

Sitting at the kitchen table a bit later, Blade and Tim dug into the cold roast chicken and ambrosia that Mattie had prepared, washing the food down with a bottle of Chardonnay. Scraping the plates and stacking them in the dishwasher, Blade suggested they turn in for the night.

"We have a long day tomorrow," Blade advised. "We've got to go to National Airport for the flight to Miami before we can board Varig for Rio."

"It'll be fine," Tim reassured her, kissing his aunt good night. "See you in the morning."

Tim went downstairs to the small basement apartment, but he wasn't ready to go to sleep; he was anticipating the adventure about to unfold the next day. He switched on the lights in the greenhouse and pulled out two clay pots. He opened the refrigerator door and took out a paper bag of narcissus bulbs. He grabbed a handful of pebbles and broken clay chips, spread them in the bottom of each pot for drainage, and carefully placed a dozen bulbs upright in each container. It was a ritual he knew as well as the Latin Mass. The bag of potting soil was split open, and Tim dug in with two fists, sprinkling mulch and dirt on top of the upright bulbs, careful to let the tips poke through. He filled the battered tin watering can and doused the pots in a generous shower, patting the dirt firmly around the protruding bulbs.

Tim stripped off his clothes, letting them drop into a pile on the floorboards in the greenhouse. He dug into the mulch bag and smeared moist dirt over his naked body, as though he were one of the bulbs he'd just planted. He moved back into the apartment toward the bathroom, turned on the hot water in the shower, and looked into the mirror above the sink at his image now being distorted on the glass by the steam from the shower. Raising a dirty hand, he traced the Kilroy image on the glass with his right pointer finger and carefully printed the name Jeffrey under the two arches etched in the mist on the mirror. The howl he let out was heard only by the stray beagle sniffing garbage cans in the ally. Tim smeared the image off the mirror and studied his reflection. He looked like a savage caveman with tears cutting paths through the grime on his cheeks.

CHAPTER 13

B lade called out down the stairway, "The car will be here in an hour! Do you want some coffee?"

"No, thanks. I'm fine," Tim yawned, wiping his eyes. He looked at the mud he had tracked into the small apartment and knew he had to do some maintenance before leaving. Mattie and Duane would come to clean later in the week, but he couldn't leave the apartment like this. He looked at the alarm clock; it was just after one o'clock. Tim had slept in all morning, and now he had to hustle to pull himself together. Fortunately, he was packed, so all he had to do was straighten up the apartment, take a shower, and shave. He got a Coke out of the small refrigerator and poured the fizzing liquid into a glass of ice. He swept the dried mud off the braided carpet onto the outdoor patio. The rug still needed to be vacuumed, but at least his muddy footprints were gone. Tim stripped the bed and folded the linens into the hamper, along with his dirty clothes from the night before. Mattie would do laundry when she came later in the week.

The town car arrived exactly on time and took Blade and Tim to the Eastern Airlines terminal for the flight to Miami. In Florida they were met at the foot of the boarding stairs by a Varig Airlines hostess wearing a white carnation.

"Good afternoon, Miss Anthony," the woman said. "I'll be escorting you and your nephew to the first-class departure lounge. If you give me your baggage claim tickets, I'll see to it that your luggage is checked through to Rio."

"Thank you," Blade said, impressed with the efficiency of the international airline. "Tim, do you have the baggage checks?"

The two were led down the airport concourse and out to the curb of the domestic arrivals section, where a limo was waiting to take them to the international terminal. Blade and Tim got in the back of the black car, and the hostess sat in the front next to the driver, checking off notes on the clipboard she carried.

The first-class lounge looked like a Knoll furniture showroom, dimly lit with sexy samba music pulsing faintly in the background. The receptionist sat in front of a gray slate wall with water rippling into a koi pond below. Two huge white orchid plants arched on either side of her, creating the scene of a jungle oasis in the middle of the commercial airport.

"Miss Anthony and her nephew, Tim Halladay," the hostess announced to the receptionist, who took the clipboard from her hand.

"Bulkhead, 1-A and 1-B," she said as she checked off a chart on her desk and then handed the clipboard back to the woman with the white carnation.

"Please make yourselves comfortable," the hostess said, pointing to leather sofas by a glass wall that overlooked the airport runway. "I'll be leaving you now. Have a wonderful flight, and thank you for choosing Varig Airlines."

Tim and Blade sank into the soft leather sofas and were immediately met by a young Brazilian waiter in tight black pants and white cummerbund, who held two glasses of champagne on a small silver tray.

"Dom Perignon, Miss Anthony?" Blade took the chilled flute and thanked the young man.

"For you, Mr. Halladay?" The boy turned, winking at Tim.

"Sure. Why not?" Tim said, toasting his aunt. The boy disappeared, probably aware that Tim was checking him out. "How does everyone know who we are and our names?" Tim asked, sipping the vintage champagne.

"Betina's friend at the Archives made these reservations. He books travel for a lot of VIPs and some high-level people in the diplomatic corps. He knows everyone. Do you mind all the attention?"

"No. Not at all. In fact, I could get used to this." Tim clinked his champagne glass against Blade's. "It's just kind of strange that they know I'm your nephew."

"Would you rather have them think you're my gigolo?" Blade purred coquettishly, the effects of the champagne starting to kick in.

"Well, we are going to Rio," Tim said, playing along.

The overnight flight to Rio was scheduled to depart at nine thirty and arrive at eight the next morning. Tim and Blade boarded with the other first-class passengers, and settled into the first row, bulkhead 1-A and 1-B.

"I don't like looking at the backs of other people's heads if I don't have to," Blade explained.

"Whatever," Tim said, rolling his eyes. "Just as long as you're comfortable."

The Varig 707 taxied onto the runway, and after a short wait, the plane was airborne and on its way to Rio. Tim and Blade reclined in the luxurious seats and were dozing off when the steward came by with dinner menus and a wine list.

"Will you be having dinner with us tonight?" the steward asked.

"Of course," Blade said, bringing her seat to the upright position. "We're here for the duration."

The leather-bound menus were like the ones presented in five-star restaurants on land. There were five main-course selections: salmon, quail, prime rib, filet mignon, and the Brazilian specialty, *feijoada*.

The entree was preceded by a selection of hors d'oeuvres: beluga caviar, shrimp, salmon, white asparagus, and hearts of palm with sauce golf. A choice of cold vichyssoise or consommé Madrilène followed.

Tim and Blade ordered the prime rib, passing on the more exotic choices. The steward left the wine list for their consideration, and then slowly eased a serving cart up the aisle with an ice sculpture of a dolphin that encased a bottle of Stolichnaya vodka and a silver seashell oozing with caviar. A circle of chilled crystal shot glasses surrounded the display, along with the chopped onion, shaved egg whites, gauze-wrapped lemon wedges, and sour cream accompaniments.

"Of course," Blade waved to the flight attendant, without being asked. "I'll have a little of everything."

"The same," Tim nodded, going along with the party.

"*Nostrovia*," Blade toasted as she downed a second shot of chilled vodka and tossed the glass over her head, sending it rolling down the aisle of the aircraft.

"Oh dear," Blade said, recovering from her sudden impulse.

"Not to worry," Tim laughed. "You missed the guy behind us," he added, referring to the Japanese businessman with eyeshades and earplugs who was sleeping soundly in the row behind them.

"Too bad," she giggled. "Imagine sleeping through all this."

"Blade," Tim said, tugging his aunt's sleeve. "Across the aisle—isn't that Pelé?"

"You mean the soccer player?" Blade asked, leaning forward to get a better view.

"Yes. The famous 'Black Pearl' who plays for Santos."

"Tim, I didn't know you were so interested in sports."

"He's only the most famous athlete in the world!"

"You may be right," Blade acknowledged. "Do you want to ask him for an autograph?"

"Of course not," Tim said, embarrassed at his aunt's suggestion.

"No, no. Of course not," Blade agreed. "It must be the vodka talking," she said and retired back into her posh reclining seat. The handsome sport icon noticed the noise across the aisle, and with a broad smile, he silently toasted Tim and Blade.

The rest of the flight was quiet and peaceful, with Blade and Tim slipping into a gentle sleep once the cabin lights had been dimmed.

Tim awoke to someone lightly tapping him on the shoulder. It was the flight attendant who'd served them spoonfuls of caviar hours before. The young man exuded a strong lemon/lime scent—English Leather cologne.

"Would you like some coffee, Mr. Halladay?" he asked, softly. "We'll be landing in Rio in one hour." He carefully lifted the shades on the three windows by Blade's seat, allowing a sliver of sunlight into the aircraft cabin, where the lights were slowly coming on to awaken the sleeping passengers.

"And Miss Anthony? May I bring her something?"

"Black tea with lemon for my aunt," Tim said.

"We have a full breakfast available," the flight attendant offered.

"Oh, please. No more food."

"Perhaps some juice. We have fresh orange, papaya, and watermelon …"

"Papaya would be great." Tim smiled at the thought of something cold and refreshing. "And ice water too, if that's possible."

"Of course it is, Mr. Halladay. Anything is possible on Varig," the flight attendant said flirtatiously.

Blade stirred in her seat, slowly blinking awake. "Are we there yet?" she asked sleepily.

Tim smiled. "The adventure is just beginning," he said, repeating his aunt's words.

Upon landing, they were whisked through immigration to a waiting Rolls-Royce that would take them to the Copacabana Palace Hotel. Along the drive from the airport, the shanties, the garbage, and the wretchedness outside looked like a backdrop from a movie. Miraculously, when they arrived, their luggage was waiting for them in the hotel lobby. A young boy in a white jockey uniform and small cap greeted them with cold hand towels as they got out of the Rolls.

"Welcome to the Copacabana Palace," a man in a dark suit and crisp white shirt said, extending a hand to greet them. He was the general manager. "Your suite is available. We'll have the luggage sent up, Miss Anthony. Please get comfortable, and let us know if there is anything we can do to make your stay more enjoyable."

"Well, that was something," Tim said, flopping down like a scarecrow on the bed in the room where his luggage had been delivered. French doors opened onto a balcony overlooking Copacabana Beach. Sheer white curtains, coaxed by a gentle ocean breeze, billowed sensuously into the room. The promenade below, a sprawling mosaic of swirling black and white tiles, resembled a marble pound cake, stretching as far as the eye could see. A continuous row of outdoor cafés lined the busy thoroughfare while hawkers with menus solicited passing tourists.

"I need a shower," Tim called out to Blade, who was getting settled in her bedroom on the other side of the suite. A room service waiter delivered a tray of bottled water, champagne, and a bowl of fresh fruit, which he set on the sideboard.

As Tim hung up the blazer he'd worn on the plane, he noticed a small envelope tucked into the inside lapel pocket. It was a card from the Varig Airlines steward, with a neatly written message: "Club Alaska, 400 Av. Atlantica, Wednesday, midnight. Fernando."

Intrigued by the cryptic invitation, Tim put the note along with his wallet, passport, and travel documents inside the wall safe in the clothes closet. He finished unpacking and then stripped off the clothes he'd been wearing for the past twenty-four hours, leaving them in a heap outside the bathroom door. He stepped into the marble stall shower, luxuriating in the cascading stream of hot water. Upon emerging ten minutes later, Tim etched the familiar graffiti figure on the misted mirror over the sink of the steam-filled bathroom. He carefully printed "Jeffrey" under the dripping image on the glass and took himself in hand to perform the familiar ritual.

A gentle tap on the door roused Tim from his sleep. He had dozed off on the bed, an oversized white bath towel draped over his body.

"Tim," his aunt's soft voice called. "Can I come in?" She entered the bedroom without waiting for an answer. "I think we might have slept right through the afternoon," she said, resting on the edge of the bed.

"Wow. It's after four o'clock," Tim said, wiping his eyes to look at the nightstand alarm clock. He pulled the bath towel over himself, aware he was naked and barely concealing a semierection.

"I think we'll have dinner here at the hotel tonight, if you don't mind," Blade suggested.

"That would be fine."

"I'll have them set up a table in a cabana by the pool. Let's say at nine o'clock. I know that's early for Brazil, but we have a big day tomorrow."

"Oh?" Tim was not aware of his aunt's plans.

"We're going to Sugar Loaf. I've booked a car to pick us up at ten. I mean, it's a must while we're here. The rest of the day we can goof off—go to the beach, shop, or whatever. But we must do some of the touristy things, if only to prove we were here."

"Sure. Whatever," Tim said, nodding. He looked out the open french doors to the soft sandy stretch of coastline that curved in a huge crescent. Foaming waves quietly unfolded on the shore, and stately palm trees stood like an endless line of soldiers in front of the modern white apartment buildings up and down the boulevard. "I think I'll take a walk on the beach. Want to come?"

"No, thank you. I'm going to take a long, hot bubble bath and then have champagne. You go ahead and explore. I'll see you for dinner," Blade said as she stood and excused herself.

Tim slipped into a pair of khaki shorts, a white T-shirt, and a pair of sandals. Since their suite was on the second floor overlooking the hotel's porte cochere, Tim took the winding marble staircase to the lobby rather than wait for an elevator.

"Stepping out for a walk, Mr. Halladay?" the front desk clerk inquired when Tim left his room key on the counter.

"I thought I'd check out the beach."

"May I suggest you leave that with us?" the young man said, pointing to the Cartier watch on Tim's wrist. "We recommend that all our guests leave valuables here when going to the beach."

"Oh," Tim said, a bit taken aback.

"Just a precaution, Mr. Halladay."

"Okay." Tim slipped off the timepiece and handed it to the young man.

Although the sun would be setting within the hour, the beach was still busy. Vendors with coolers slung over their shoulders patrolled up and down the sand, offering cold bottled water, soft drinks, and ice cream. A spirited volleyball game was in full swing, the players a team of perfectly shaped almond-colored boys wearing only Speedos.

Tim removed his sandals, holding them over his shoulder, and dug his toes into the wet sand along the shore, letting warm lapping waves wash over his legs and dampen his shorts. Bending over to cup a handful of salt water to splash on his face, Tim became aware that he wasn't alone in the surf: a gang of children, boys who couldn't have been more than five or six years old, had surrounded him. A few were holding what looked like sharpened wooden ice cream sticks. The leader of the unruly pack was shouting, "*Cruzeiros, cruzeiros!*" As if to emphasize his demand, the boy slashed his wooden weapon across Tim's right arm, drawing blood.

Infuriated, Tim swung his other arm, still holding the sandals, in a wide arc in front of the kids, shouting, "Get away from me, you brats!" That sent the scruffy mob splashing into the surf, laughing. In a minute they were gone, running down the beach to harass their next victim.

Tim was annoyed he had been such an obvious tourist target. Licking the bleeding scratch, which had splattered his white T-shirt and khaki shorts, he plodded through the wide expanse of sand to the promenade on Av. Atlantica. He stopped at the first café on the other side of the crosswalk and let a hawker escort him to a small sidewalk table. Although he had left all his valuables at the hotel, Tim had had the foresight to slip his American Express card into the hip pocket of his shorts. He didn't care if the tourist prices in the café were ridiculously inflated; he just wanted to sit back and lick his wound—literally. He ordered a local beer and olives.

"I see you've been to the beach," the waiter said with a wink when he set down Tim's order.

"Yes," Tim answered, flushing with embarrassment.

"They're just beggars," the waiter said. "Only they can get aggressive sometimes."

"No kidding."

A few minutes later, an old man approached Tim. *"Apartamento, temporare?"* he whispered. "Twenty dollars. For one hour," he said, pointing to a scrawny barefoot boy at his side. The kid, with haunting brown eyes and decayed teeth, may have been ten years old.

"No! No," Tim said, disgusted, waving aside the old man and gesturing to the waiter for a check. A woman draped in layers of postcards immediately stepped up, pointing to pictures of the Corcovado Christ statue on Sugar Loaf.

"No, thank you." Tim abruptly signed the credit card receipt without checking the total. He dashed into the street, the woman with postcards following behind. He was running and out of breath by the time he reached the Copacabana Palace Hotel.

"Welcome back, Mr. Halladay," the doorman said, noticing Tim's bloodstained T-shirt.

"It's nice to be back," Tim said curtly, approaching the front desk to get his room key and retrieve his watch.

Blade was sitting on the sofa when he quietly let himself into the suite. She was dressed in a stunning cream linen pantsuit, thumbing through a copy of *Vogue Italia* and sipping champagne.

"How was the beach?" she asked, glancing up at her nephew. She looked startled upon seeing the blood on his T-shirt.

"More local color than I would have asked for on my first day in Rio."

"Champagne?" Blade asked, deciding not to make an issue of his appearance.

"No. I'm going to have scotch." Tim headed for the well-stocked bar and poured himself a tumbler of Dewar's. He sat down in an oversized armchair opposite his aunt and proceeded to tell her about his encounter with the ruffians on the beach. He decided to omit the incident with the old man attempting to sell him a boy, thinking that was more local color than Blade needed to absorb.

Dinner was elegant but casual. A table had been set in a poolside cabana. Hundreds of vigil light candles flickered around the Olympic-size pool, and the cabana's canvas drapes had been partly closed for privacy. They ordered hearts of palm with sauce golf, followed by grilled local whitefish and baby boiled potatoes sprinkled with parsley butter. A chilled bottle of Pouilly-Fuissé complemented the dinner.

"I don't know how I can ever repay or even thank you for all you've done for me," Tim said, feeling the effects of the fragrant white wine.

"Tickets to your opening night on Broadway would be good," Blade said as she raised her glass in a toast, trying to avoid serious conversation.

"You know what I mean."

"I do know, Tim," Blade said softly, resting her hand on top of his. "But tomorrow's a full day, and I think we should turn in."

The next morning the Mercedes was in the porte cochere promptly at ten.

"*Bom dia*, Miss Anthony," the driver said as he unfolded a cold towel with a flourish and handed it to her. "And for you, Mr. Halladay."

"Thank you," they replied in unison.

"I'm Hector," the driver said, retrieving the used towels. "I'll be with you all day. First we go to Sugar Loaf and Corcovado. Then, afterward, anywhere you would like. I will be your guide and your protector." He smiled, reassuring his American passengers as they settled back into the Mercedes. Traffic on Av. Atlantica was frenzied, a cacophony of horns, buses spewing putrid diesel fumes, and people hanging out of the windows to breathe polluted air. Motor scooters holding two or three adults, often with a child hanging on, buzzed through the snarled traffic like angry hornets. Tim and Blade sank into the comfortable leather backseat of the German car, insulated from the world outside, air-conditioning on full blast.

"We're here," Hector announced as he pulled the Mercedes into a parking area at the base of the tram leading up to gumdrop-shaped Pao De Acucar, Sugar Loaf Mountain. "I'll be right back." And with that, Hector was out of the car, speaking to a policeman, who took him to the front of a long line of people waiting to buy tickets.

In minutes Hector returned and opened the door of the Mercedes. "Right there, Miss Anthony." He gestured to a turnstile a short distance away where a guard was taking tickets from visitors cued up to board the tram up Sugar Loaf. The ride offered panoramic views of the modern city below, views of pristine beaches with cruise ships docked in the distance, and a bird's-eye look at the famous Cristo Redentor statue on nearby Corcovado, Hunchback Mountain. "You can stop halfway up at Urca. There is a café where you can rest, have a coffee, and take pictures before going up to the top. I will be here waiting when you get back."

The short walk to the turnstile was lined with hawkers selling postcards, T-shirts, and tacky souvenirs. A photographer busily took pictures of the tourists as they boarded the waiting gondolas.

On the ride back down the mountain, Blade clasped Tim's arm as he hung way out of the cable car, taking pictures of the magnificent horizon of royal blue Atlantic waves kissing the white crescent beaches. "I know it's touristy, which you hate, but we had to do it," Blade apologized.

"Of course we did," Tim smirked. "When in Rome."

"You're so bad," Blade chided.

"That's why you love me."

As Tim and Blade gingerly stepped out of the swaying gondola, they were approached by the photographer who'd been taking pictures of them on their way up the mountain. He was offering postcards, photo albums, and a decorative plate with images of them wearing sunglasses, seemingly waving into the camera. Actually, they had been trying to fend off the annoying photographer, but the resulting photos looked quite different.

"Here," Blade said, slipping a wad of *cruzeiros* into Tim's hand. "Buy that hideous plate."

"You must be joking." Tim was astounded at his aunt's suggestion.

"Do you think I want that thing showing up in some garage sale—or worse yet, in *Women's Wear Daily*? Blade Anthony on holiday in Rio! Just buy it."

"I'm going to keep this as a treasured souvenir of our trip to South America," Tim laughed as the two drove away in the back of the Mercedes. He unfolded the newspaper wrapped around the plate and held it up in mock admiration, as Hector peered over his shoulder in amazement at his giggling passengers. They spent the rest of the afternoon exploring antique shops and small galleries on Rua Barata. They ended up in Ipanema, strolling past trendy boutiques pulsating with American disco music. Blade insisted on buying Tim a new T-shirt to replace the bloodied one from his beach excursion the day before. But at one hundred US dollars, he was shocked at the extravagance, although it did fit him like a second skin and was the softest material he had ever placed against his body.

The next day was shopping for Blade. Hector picked them up again at ten in the morning. After a brief stop at the H. Stern boutique off the lobby at the Copacabana Palace, where a woman dressed in a dark suit gave Blade a card of introduction, they left for the headquarters of the famed gem seller on Rua Visconde de Pirajá. Hector didn't need directions; he'd driven wealthy clients there many times before. Blade was looking for an emerald, and she vacillated between H. Stern and the Amsterdam-Sauer Company, insisting that Hector drive back and forth between the two jewelers before she could make a final decision.

"I know you're bored," she said to Tim, who'd patiently escorted his aunt on her quest for the perfect gem. "But look at this specimen," Blade gushed as she fondled the glistening emerald she had purchased. "I'm going to have it mounted in a simple cocktail ring setting—elegant but understated."

"I thought you might put it in a tiara and wear it to the next formal ball at the Congressional Country Club," Tim teased.

"You are incorrigible." Blade poked her nephew in the ribs. "But you know, that's not a bad idea," she laughed.

"Just don't wear it to any fundraisers with John Hartwell, or you may have to mortgage Thirty-Third Street."

To show appreciation for her nephew's patience in putting up with her day of shopping, Blade took him to an extravagant dinner at Le Bec Fin, a venerable French restaurant in the Copacabana district. The next day would be, as though promised in a tour brochure, a day at leisure, with no activities planned. Blade sensed that her nephew might like some time on his own, without feeling an obligation to entertain his aunt. She also welcomed time to pamper herself: to lounge in a cabana by the hotel pool and get a relaxing massage from one of the tanned boys in white shorts who worked at the health club.

Tim left the hotel at ten that evening, early for a night out in Rio, so he strolled slowly down the black and white mosaic-tiled Av. Atlantica, careful to avoid being swept into a sidewalk café luring tourists for an overpriced beer—or a rent boy.

Tim had told Blade about the invitation from the Varig steward, and she'd encouraged him to go to the club, while cautioning him to be careful. He walked slowly down the busy promenade in his new hundred-dollar T-shirt from the Ipanema boutique and a tight pair of Levis. It was a balmy, moonlit night, with palm trees gently waving in a sensuous breeze overhead. The mood changed on Av. Atlantica as the street numbers on the blocks descended. Luxurious apartment buildings and international hotels gave way to malls and *danceterias* pumping out loud music. Tim knew he was heading in the right direction when he heard "Can't Take My Eyes Off of You" by Frankie Valli blaring from a sidewalk club packed with shirtless boys dancing. He checked the card from the airline steward to verify the address: "Club Alaska, 400 Av. Atlantica," which, if he were reading the street numbers correctly, should be the next block.

A twenty-four-hour pharmacy and a cheap shoe store marked the spot on the block where Tim calculated the club should be. He was about to give up and head back to the hotel when he was approached by a muscled guy in leather chaps. "Club Alaska?"

"Yes," Tim answered. "Do you know where it is?"

"Up the stairs," the guy said, pointing. "It's hard to find if you don't know."

"Thanks. I'm supposed to meet someone there."

"Sure, kid," the guy smirked. "Have a good time."

Tim paid the cover charge at the door and in return had his wrist stamped with a black letter "A" that glowed under the strobe lights in the disco. The dance hall was cavernous and mobbed with young, shirtless men dancing. Four cell-like cages were suspended from the ceiling just over the heads of the dancers. In each cage a go-go boy wearing only a black string thong gyrated to the throbbing music, mostly American and British rock, interspersed with an occasional disco version of a Brazilian samba. Clouds of pot smoke, interlaced with amyl nitrate, permeated the dance floor, as boys dancing in groups or by themselves got lost in the euphoria.

Tim managed to push his way through the sweaty crowd to a long bar at the back of the disco, where he ordered a beer. The bartender, a pretty blond Brazilian wearing only a thong like the caged dancing boys, smiled. "American?"

"Am I that obvious?" Tim grinned self-consciously.

"You're cute," the bartender flirted, turning to give Tim a full view of his perfectly shaped butt. "Welcome to Club Alaska."

"I see you found it," a voice from behind said. It was Fernando, the wine steward from Varig. "And I see you're making friends," he said, nodding his head at the blond bartender.

"Hey there!" Tim was happy to see a familiar face but oblivious to his comment. "This is quite a place."

"I thought you'd like it," Fernando said, touching Tim's hand. "We all come here." He gestured to two boys beside him who had been on the flight from Miami to Rio. "This is Pepe and Rico." Turning to introduce Tim, he said, "This is Mr. Halladay from 1-A."

"Nice to meet you." Tim shook both boys' hands. "I mean, off the airplane."

"Your aunt, Miss Anthony? She let you out?" Fernando pressed.

"She's cool." Tim said.

"We had a bet on the plane whether she was *really* your aunt," Fernando confided.

"You mean ... you thought there was something going on?" Tim burst into laughter.

"I knew I was right," Fernando boasted to his two friends. "He's much too sweet to be a gigolo." He gently squeezed Tim's cheeks. "Do you want to dance?" Without waiting for a response, Fernando eased Tim onto the dance floor, along with Pepe and Rico, whose bodies were already glistening with sweat, their shirts abandoned. A long draw of amyl nitrate from the silver bullet inhaler around Rico's neck sent Tim into closed-eye abandon as he danced to "Close Your Eyes" by Peaches and Herb.

It was after four o'clock when Tim and the three flight attendants stumbled out of Club Alaska and into the deserted shopping mall below. Fernando slid away to the all-night pharmacy, while Tim, held up like a limp ragdoll by Pepe and Rico, succumbed helplessly, giddily watching streetlights pass by overhead from inside the backseat of a taxi.

Harsh sunlight seeped in through half-closed drapes above a whirring air-conditioning unit that dripped water in the window. Tim was in an apartment, somewhere. He was naked on an unmade bed with Pepe and Rico, also naked, hugging him like bookends. The back of his neck throbbed as though it would explode. His vision was blurred. Remnants of the previous night's party littered the sparsely furnished room: half-squeezed tubes of K-Y, inhalers, and small open bottles of liquid amyl, as well as crumpled towels and remnants of joints.

Tim looked up at the stained acoustic ceiling tiles, took a deep breath, and slowly extricated himself from the arms of the naked, sleeping flight attendants. He found his jeans and the expensive T-shirt Blade had bought him the day before. His shoes were nowhere in sight. Fernando was fully clothed, snoring on a sofa in the small living room. Tim wanted to say thank you or good-bye or something, but putting his Fairfield County good manners aside, he let himself silently out of the apartment and took the elevator to the lobby, where a weary doorman was smoking a cigarette.

"Do you want a taxi?" the man asked.

"I need to get to the Copacabana Palace Hotel."

"You can walk," the doorman said, looking down at Tim's bare feet. "It's ten blocks. Faster than the afternoon traffic."

"Afternoon?" Tim realized he had no idea what time it was.

"It's just after one," the doorman said, checking his watch.

"Shit!" Tim blurted out, realizing that Blade must be worried about him by this time. "Which way?"

The doorman pointed indifferently and then sat down on a stool by the front door, picking up his newspaper and rolling his eyes.

Tim quickly got his bearings and realized he was only two blocks from Av. Atlantica in the general vicinity of Club Alaska. The walk back to the hotel would take about fifteen minutes. He tried to walk in the shade since the black and white mosaic tiles on the promenade burned his bare feet.

The doorman greeted him as though a disheveled and barefoot guest returning in the early afternoon was completely normal. "Welcome back, Mr. Halladay," he said. Tim brushed by the man without speaking, retrieved his key from the front desk, and quietly let himself into the suite on the second floor.

Blade was on the balcony, sipping an espresso. The room service tray from breakfast was on the coffee table in the sitting room, having sat there uncollected for some time. The "Do Not Disturb" sign was posted on the door, so the suite had not been serviced. Through the open door, Tim saw that his bed was untouched, turned down with a chocolate on the pillow.

"I'm sorry, Blade. I—"

"I hope you had a good time," she said, cutting him off.

"I should have called," he said apologetically.

"Nonsense. You know the rules."

"Rules?" Tim asked, confused.

"There are no rules," she said with a wink, hugging her nephew.

CHAPTER 14

Checking out of the Copacabana Palace was as grand an affair as their arrival. Blade and Tim were met in the lobby by the general manager, who escorted them to a waiting Rolls-Royce, this time driven by Hector. Tim was still feeling sick from his debaucheries of the night before. He gazed out the tinted windows of the luxury car. Ragged children pressed against the vehicle, smudging the windows with greasy fingers, begging for *cruzeiros*. Tim was ready to leave Brazil, and when Hector pulled up to the curbside check-in at PanAm for the flight to Montevideo, he was relieved to see the blue-and-white uniforms of the airline staff.

It was off-season in Uruguay, but Blade had made arrangements for them to stay at a stone country farmhouse in Punta del Este, a beachside resort an hour's drive from Montevideo, on the Atlantic coast. A German couple ran the inn, listed as a Relais & Chateaux in the guidebooks, and during peak season it was easily the most expensive resort in Uruguay, attracting a clientele of international movie stars, diplomats, and even drug dealers.

A diesel Mercedes taxi picked them up at the airport in Montevideo, and soon, they were pulling up through open gates onto the gravel drive at the entrance of the farmhouse. "You know, Miss Anthony," the owner said when they arrived, "we are not really open. But when we received the telegram from Washington, of course we would make room for you and your nephew."

"Thank you," Blade said appreciatively. "My late husband and I were in Punta del Este many years ago, and I wanted Tim to see how beautiful and peaceful it is here. Especially after a week in Rio." Blade glanced knowingly at Tim.

"Yes, I remember. I believe you were on your wedding trip."

"That's right," Blade replied, amazed at the man's memory.

The restaurant was closed for the season, but the owner's wife made a simple chicken and rice dinner that the four ate in the kitchen. Two bottles of Uruguayan merlot completed the meal. Afterward, the owner insisted on treating his guests to a brandy in the bar atop the stone water tower—the center of the old farmhouse. The structure resembled a lighthouse, with a twisting metal staircase leading to the top level and a cozy upstairs bar with four stools. From there guests could enjoy an unobstructed view of the sand dunes and deserted beach that stretched for miles along the Atlantic Coast.

"It looks like East Hampton meets Beverly Hills," Tim commented, looking out over the boarded-up mansions along the beach.

Meanwhile, the owner had switched on a two-way radio, broadcasting in German from Berlin. "I can only get reception up here," he explained, tuning in to the static-laced transmission.

Blade looked at Tim, reading his mind. She had told him of rumors she'd heard that there were Nazis living in South America, in addition to the scores of refugees who had fled there after the war. "Don't even go there," she whispered to Tim before he could comment. "Remember where we are." She inhaled a long sniff of the smoky brandy.

As prearranged, the old diesel Mercedes taxi rattled up the gravel driveway to the farmhouse at ten the next morning, and the driver, dressed in a shabby but clean uniform, patiently waited for the travelers. The German innkeeper and the driver struggled with the luggage, which, after a few attempts, the two men managed to cram into the trunk and front seat of the Mercedes.

"You must come back during the season, Miss Anthony," the German owner said apologetically, wiping his forehead with a handkerchief. "January is wonderful, and everyone is here from Buenos Aires. We are fully staffed then, and the restaurant is open. We will prepare a splendid meal for you."

"Dinner in the kitchen last night was lovely. Just what we needed after a hectic time in Rio," Blade said, taking the man's hand. "Please be sure to thank your wife for us."

"You are too kind, Miss Anthony."

Blade and Tim got into the backseat of the Mercedes and waved good-bye to the German innkeeper as the car pulled out of the driveway and onto the two-lane highway back toward Montevideo. Blade had decided to bypass the large capital city and proceed on to Colonia, a two-and-a-half-hour drive along the Rio de la Plata, the wide river separating Uruguay and Argentina. Colonia was a port city, originally settled by the Portuguese in the seventeenth century. The old section retained much of its colonial architecture, but the importance of the city was its role as the gateway to Buenos Aires across the river. From Colonia, Blade and Tim would take a hydrofoil to the final destination on their South American adventure.

It was early evening when the taxi transporting Blade and Tim from the ferry terminal pulled into the circular cobblestone drive in front of the Claridge Hotel in Buenos Aires. With four stately white Ionic columns gracing the facade, the Claridge looked more like a formal government building than a four-star hotel.

"It's not the Plaza," Blade said, referring to the famous old hotel on the Plaza San Martín where she had stayed with Joseph Dilorio on their honeymoon, "but the service is better, and the rooms are comfortable, if a bit tired."

"This looks quite fine," Tim said as he emerged from the taxi and was presented with a cold hand towel by a boy dressed in an impeccable white uniform.

"Welcome to the Claridge Hotel, Mr. Halladay," the boy said cheerfully.

Tim turned to his aunt. "How does everyone always know our name?"

"It's because we're nice people," Blade teased, giving no other explanation for the extraordinary service they'd received everywhere since leaving Washington a week before. The reception at the front desk was equally gracious.

"We have you in a suite on the twelfth floor," the manager explained, escorting Blade and Tim to the elevator. "It's the only one with a private terrace."

That evening they had dinner at the hotel, in the long, formal wood-paneled dining room off the lobby that was decidedly British in atmosphere.

"Tomorrow I want to take you to San Telmo," Blade announced, sensing Tim's disappointment with the conservative, dull environment of the Claridge. "It's the oldest section of the city with many antique shops and wonderful buildings. There's a flea market, but I think only on Sunday."

The next morning they took a taxi to Plaza Dorrego in the San Telmo district, where the antique shops were just opening. Blade and Tim ordered espresso in a dusty tango bar on the square where a fat orange tabby cat was stretched out asleep in the open window. The proprietor was hosing down the crumbling sidewalk and watering geraniums in the window box, careful not to disturb the purring feline. Blade and Tim sipped the strong coffee as bells in the neighboring church rang the noon hour.

The windows of the shops were filled with copper maritime instruments, telescopes, elegant dolls, puppets, and old phonographs with large horn-shaped listening devices. They stepped into a corner shop where they were barely able to navigate the crammed aisles. The mustachioed owner was listening to a scratchy Enrico Caruso recording of *La Boheme* and looked not at all impressed by his American visitors. Tim began poking through a stack of out-of-print *porteño* magazines from the turn of the century, intrigued by the black-and-white prewar photos of European cities. In an adjoining display case, tiny metal soldiers, many in Nazi uniforms, marched in formation in front of model tanks and warships. In the display case glass Tim detected an image, a reflection of someone looking into the shop from the street outside. He turned, but there was no one there. He pulled a ballpoint pen from inside his jacket pocket and crouched down out of sight. He scribbled the arched image with almond-shaped eyes and the familiar "Jeffrey Was Here" signature in the corner of the display case glass where he'd seen the reflection moments before.

Blade was captivated by a collection of antique perfume bottles and had picked up a graceful Lalique in the shape of a calla lily.

"What do you think?" she asked Tim, holding up the glass flower in her palm.

"It's beautiful," Tim said, distracted by a large model ship in the case behind his aunt. A three-stack wooden ship, over three feet in length—part warship, with toy cannons mounted on the deck, but part passenger liner, with portholes on the hull—floated mysteriously in the display case behind Blade. Blue-and-white paper Argentine flags flew from its rigging. Sensing her nephew's fixation, Blade turned to inspect.

"It's quite something," she commented.

"Not for sale," the shop owner said as he approached. "It's for display only."

"Then why do you have it in the shop?" Blade asked.

"Signora, it's for everyone to enjoy," the man replied officiously. "You see, it is only finished on one side," he pointed out. The reverse side of the ship model was painted but had no portholes or detail of any kind. "It was made for a department store in Buenos Aires in 1920, after the war," he explained. "It was only meant to be in the storefront window for display."

"And the price?" Blade pressed.

"I'm sorry. It is not for sale."

Tim looked disappointed but was comforted by his find of the premiere edition of *Holiday* magazine from March 1946, in excellent condition, an unlikely discovery in this part of the world. The shop owner obviously did not appreciate its significance because he sold it to Tim for fifty cents, apparently thinking only a stupid American would pay so much for an out-of-date travel magazine.

"Do you still want the Lalique?" the shop owner asked Blade, who did and bought it.

During the taxi ride back to the Claridge Hotel, the two inspected their purchases: Tim was fascinated by the United Airlines ad in *Holiday* magazine promoting its soon-to-come four-engine "five-mile-a-minute" Mainliner service, and the Studebaker car ad promising "trustworthy father-and-son craftsmanship." Blade pressed the Lalique calla lily softly against her cheek as she stared out the taxi window at the passing colonial houses with their imposing wooden doors and bronze, lion-headed handles.

Dinner that night at Clark's was a tradition that Blade wished to preserve from her first memory there with Joseph Dilorio. She ordered an entire suckling baby pig, *los cochinillos de Clark's*, a house specialty, even when Tim winced at the idea of eating a young animal.

"It's marvelous," Blade said, putting her hand on Tim's as the wine steward uncorked a bottle of Mendoza cabernet.

"I don't know." Tim grinned and sipped the deep red wine. "I don't feel comfortable eating anything called 'baby.'"

"You'll get used to it." Blade toasted her nephew with a goblet of the full-bodied wine. "It's an acquired taste," she said before drifting off into her own thoughts.

After a long silence, Tim asked, "Do you ever think of Jeffrey?"

"Of course I do," Blade said, refusing to be caught off guard.

"I just wondered."

"What do you want to know?" Blade asked, looking at Tim kindly. "I knew we would eventually have this conversation, but I didn't think it would be over baby pig in Argentina," she added, trying to lighten the mood.

"I mean, no one ever told me anything," Tim said.

"To protect you, Tim. That's all. No one wanted you to be hurt." Blade was trying to offer an explanation but knew she had faltered.

"Protect me from the truth?" Tim said flatly. "They must have known I would find out someday."

"Well! What do you want to know?" Blade asked, refusing to let her nephew control the situation.

Flustered but not deterred by his aunt's directness, Tim started to ask the questions he'd been harboring for years. "Who was born first? Me or Jeffrey?"

"You were," Blade said flatly. "At 11:52 p.m."

"When was Jeffrey born?"

Blade hesitated, taking another sip of the strong red wine. "Jeffrey was born fifteen minutes later. He was breathing, but only for a short time. They tried everything to keep him alive, but it was hopeless. He only lived a few minutes before he was pronounced legally dead."

"So we would have been born on two different days," Tim calculated.

"Yes, technically. I suppose so."

"Where is he buried?" Tim asked.

"There is a small marker in Riverside Cemetery in Norwalk, next to your grandparents' grave."

"Can we go there sometime?"

"Of course. But why?" Blade asked.

"Because I've always been a little in love with death."

"You got an A in that O'Neill class, didn't you?" Blade said, picking up on the reference to the depressing playwright. "If I tell you what you want to hear," Blade pressed, "will you stop the graffiti?"

"You know?" Tim looked up, fully aware of the answer.

"Everyone does," Blade answered softly. "But why do you do it?"

"It's been my only connection since no one would tell me about him, like keeping a part of me secret and away from me."

"That was probably a mistake," Blade mused. "We all just wanted what was best for you. Funny, when we try to protect the ones we love, how often we end up hurting them instead."

"I know you meant well."

"The doctor said you two would have been identical," Blade confided. "Imagine … two of you!"

"Yes, imagine," Tim thought aloud as he looked out to the crowded dining room, beyond the baby piglet, an apple in its mouth, on the carving board alongside the table.

The morning edition of the *International Herald Tribune* blazed an unusually large-type headline the next day: "ISRAEL–SYRIA AT WAR."

"This is certainly disturbing," Blade commented as she dissolved a sugar cube in her coffee. The buffet breakfast at the Claridge had been set for a hundred guests, although barely a dozen were seated in the formal wood-paneled dining room. "And now Egypt and Jordan are involved," Blade observed as she read the newspaper. "This can't be good for any of us."

"Did you forget about that little thing called Vietnam?" Tim remarked sarcastically.

"I'm sorry." Blade looked up. "I know you are concerned about all that, but there is nothing we can do."

"Just sit here in the dining room of a posh hotel in Buenos Aires worrying about the crisis while the world flies by." Surprised by his bitterness, Tim immediately apologized. "I'm sorry. I'm just a bit on edge."

"Of course you are," Blade said sympathetically. Changing the subject, she said, "I thought we'd go to Recoleta this morning. A good cemetery might cheer you up."

Tim broke out in a big grin, easing the tension. "You know me too well."

Soon they were in a taxi, on their way. "Of course, everyone wants to see Evita," Blade announced as they drove toward the famous cemetery.

"But hers is actually one of the least interesting of the mausoleums. You will see when we get there."

Outside the brick walls of the cemetery, a horse-drawn carriage transported huge flower arrangements for a funeral scheduled later that morning. The gates opened at ten, in a little less than an hour, allowing time for Blade and Tim to have an espresso at an outdoor café.

"You know, you can rent one of the tombs for a funeral, have the body enshrined for a month or so, and then have it removed for final burial or disposal elsewhere. The concierge told me when I said we wanted to go to Recoleta."

"Sounds very Hollywood," Tim laughed. "Did the concierge think we were here to put someone away?"

"No, I'm sure not. But he did say we were in for a treat this morning."

"Oh?" Tim was intrigued.

"Yes. There is a burial in the crypt of the Lavalle family, an Argentine dynasty dating back for generations."

A parade of limousines, accompanied by policemen on motorcycles, pulled up slowly to the main iron gate of Recoleta, which was just opening. A horse-drawn caisson bearing a coffin covered with hundreds of cascading white roses followed. A gaudy purple satin ribbon with the name Lavalle in gold letters hung over the elegant blooms. Tim and Blade took places at the end of the line of mourners and followed the procession to the open mausoleum.

"Blade," Tim said quietly, tugging at his aunt's sleeve. "I think we're being watched."

"What?" she asked, momentarily distracted from the solemnity of the proceedings.

"That policeman." Tim nodded over his shoulder.

Blade turned, squinting to see who her nephew was talking about. "Who? I don't see anyone."

"There," Tim said, pointing as the pallbearers slowly glided the flower-laden coffin into the chapel. The policeman wasn't there now, but Tim was certain it was the same man whose reflection he had seen in the display case in the antique shop the day before.

A Catholic priest read the graveside prayers in Spanish, and as quickly as they had descended, the mourners in the funeral procession dispersed into their waiting limousines outside the cemetery gate, leaving the coffin in the open chapel with rows of flickering candles in jars around the crypt. A young girl with a broken straw broom swept up fallen rose petals and cigarette butts left by the crowd. Workmen from the cemetery would come later to seal the tomb until another Lavalle joined the resting place. Tim quietly approached and picked up a small white rosebud that had fallen onto the cobblestone entrance to the gravesite.

"That was quite something," Tim said, smelling the delicate flower.

"Do you still want to see Evita?"

"Sure, but I think it will be a letdown after that."

They wandered the rows of ornate tombs, many boasting sculpted marble angels, obelisks, and statues of Christ and various saints. It appeared that the gravesites were in competition to see which could be more ostentatious. Many were small replicas of chapels, complete with altars, crucifixes, and gold candelabra, all sheltered behind stained-glass windows. Following directions from the concierge, Blade and Tim found the nondescript site they were looking for: a simple black stone marker with the name "Peron." A glass jar of dead daisies sat forlornly at the base of the crypt, and dandelion weeds grew in the cracks of the surrounding cement.

"Not exactly Lavalle," Tim commented.

Later that afternoon, they strolled down Florida, a busy shopping area lined with small shops, a huge department store, and several popular *confeteria*. They started their shopping foray at the beginning of Florida, where the venerable Plaza Hotel sat haughtily facing Plaza San Martín.

"I've made reservations for us tonight at the Grill Room," Blade announced, pointing to the Plaza. "You'll have to wear a blazer and tie, but it's a must and worth it. The president often entertains foreign guests in the dining room. It's like a private club, and definitely *not* for tourists."

"Of course," Tim teased. "I'm sure that's how you got us in. But please, no more baby animals."

Blade dragged Tim into an exclusive fur shop, by appointment only, off Plaza San Martín, where they spent two hours looking at expensive pelts and hides.

"Do you like the vicuña?" Blade asked, referring to the soft, apricot-colored fur that was strewn across the oriental carpet in front of her, along with several other rare skins.

"It's beautiful, but you know that it's an endangered species."

"Yes, of course. But this one is already dead, and there is nothing I can do to save it."

"Your reasoning is amazing," Tim said, shrugging.

Blade nodded to the saleswoman to wrap the vicuña and have it delivered to the Claridge Hotel.

"I just don't want to be in customs when you're trying to get that through," Tim commented.

Guido's, an Italian-owned leather emporium on Florida, was the next stop. Tim looked at the dress shoes, belts, and elegant luggage in the outside display windows before entering the shop. Blade insisted that Tim be fitted for a pair of Oxford wing tips, which would be delivered to the Claridge the next day.

"Thank you," Tim said as they exited the shop out onto busy Florida. "I think I'm going back to the hotel to take a nap before dinner."

Blade touched her nephew's arm as the two walked toward the hotel. "You are fun to travel with," she said, tightening her grip. "I'm going to have tea in the lobby while you rest. Just plan to be ready by nine. I have some cards to write and a few other things to attend to."

Tim slept longer than he'd planned. The room was dark when he woke up sprawled out on the bed, still in his street clothes. Soft music was coming from the sitting room, and light crept into his room from under the closed door. He looked at the bedside alarm clock and was relieved to see that it was only eight—plenty of time for him to revive and dress for dinner at the Plaza Grill Room. He stripped and turned the water on in the shower, calling out to Blade through the closed door, "I'll be out in a few minutes!"

When Tim stepped back out of the shower, he wiped the steam off the mirror above the bathroom sink and looked at his reflection, beads of perspiration running down his cheeks. His aunt's words haunted him: "Imagine … two of you!"

Dressing quickly, he unfolded his blazer on the bed and opened the door to join Blade in the sitting room, only to stop abruptly. He just barely caught himself before he tripped over the large object blocking the doorway.

Tim gasped. "What the … ?"

"Your ship has come in," Blade announced grandly.

The model ship from the antique shop in San Telmo—half warship/half passenger liner and completed on only one side—rested at the doorway to Tim's room.

"You've got to be kidding."

"I had to do something to make up for your displeasure with the vicuña."

"But it wasn't for sale."

"Nonsense. This is Argentina," Blade said dismissively. "But we are going to be something in customs."

Dinner at the Plaza Grill Room lived up to Blade's predictions. Although the president was not dining there that evening, several high-ranking officers from the military were holding court with a group of Middle Eastern businessmen dressed in white caftans. Cuban cigars and thirty-year-old brandy flowed freely. Two young boys in Moroccan attire were seated on pillows at either end of the dining room, slowly pulling back and forth on an overhead tapestry fan, creating a soft breeze that dissipated the cigar smoke. The sommelier, looking like a wooden puppet from *The Nutcracker*, decanted the Mendoza pinot noir that Blade had ordered to accompany their rack of lamb dinner.

"This is really something," Tim said, toasting his aunt. "I mean the whole trip has been wonderful."

"Didn't you say that you knew places to go for entertainment?" Blade probed diplomatically.

"M gave me the name of a club he thought I might find interesting," Tim acknowledged. "I looked it up. It's not too far from the Claridge."

"I think you might want to go there after dinner. Spending too much time with your aunt might become a bit stifling after a while."

"Never," Tim said, quickly cutting her off. "You know I love spending time with you."

"Yes, but there are times …" Blade let the thought drift unfinished.

The Café Einstein was a ten-minute walk from the Claridge, past Florida, tucked into an alley behind the Colon Theatre. M had warned that it might be hard to find, with no sign and with taxi drivers refusing to acknowledge its existence. It was one of many popular emerging concert cafés, small avant-garde salons hidden in cellars or the back rooms of restaurants, where singers and musicians performed for enthusiastic audiences of young bohemians.

A man smoking a cigarette appeared to be standing guard in a doorway lit by a single exposed light bulb overhead.

"Einstein?" Tim asked under his breath as the man checked him out suspiciously. Tim had changed into jeans and his Ipanema T-shirt and put on his tight black leather jacket, unbuttoned, all in a concerted effort to not look like a tourist.

The man took a long drag on his cigarette, stared Tim in the eye, and nodded silently toward a wooden stairway leading to the second floor of a building that looked abandoned. Soft guitar music grew louder as Tim ascended the creaky stairs. He slipped into a smoke-filled room where hundreds of candles burned in empty beer, Chianti, and Mateus rosé bottles. Wax from burning candles dripped onto the wooden floor and on the few beer-keg tables inside the cramped room. Young people, mostly pretty Argentine boys, sat in groups on the floor, arms and legs entwined, listening to a blond guitar player singing American folk songs.

Tim was handed a beer, without asking, by a dark-haired boy in a tank top. "American?"

"I was hoping it wasn't so obvious," Tim said, accepting the drink with a smile.

"We don't get many in here," the boy flirted. "Where are you from?"

"Washington," Tim answered. "I'm here with my aunt on holiday."

"How did you find Café Einstein?" the boy questioned. "Certainly not from the hotel concierge."

"No. A friend going to Georgetown told me about this place. He said I should check it out."

"Emerson?" the boy asked with a wink.

"You know him?" Tim's eyes widened in surprise.

"I got a postcard saying I should look out for a cute American who was coming to Argentina. But he didn't tell me what a dreamboat you were."

"So you know Emerson?"

"Everyone knows M," the boy said. "I hope that's not a problem."

"No. Of course not. We're friends."

"Good," the boy said, patting Tim on the butt. "I get off at four," he added seductively, "if you're up to it."

Tim mingled with the crowd, sitting on the floor next to boys who were holding hands.

The blond Argentine singer strummed his guitar and sang "If I Had a Hammer" and "We Shall Overcome" as those sitting around him swayed to the lyrics. After his third beer, still not having had to pay for drinks, Tim stumbled up, cramped from sitting cross-legged so long, looked at his watch, and saw that it was almost four o'clock, quitting time for the waiter.

Outside it was chilly as Tim zipped up the front of his leather jacket. He decided to pass on the waiter's vague invitation, preferring to walk back to the Claridge alone. He passed under the tiered wedding-cake facade of the Colon Theatre and back up Florida. The streets were deserted, and a cold mist hung in the night air. He stopped in front of the Guido shoe emporium where his custom-made Oxford wing tips would be ready later in the day. He looked at his reflection in the glass window only to realize he was not alone. Tim turned around slowly. There was a real person standing in front of him and not a stranger passing on a deserted Buenos Aires street, but his actual double image. The two stood frozen, staring at each other. Neither spoke.

Tim started to move, but the figure held up his right hand to stop him. Their eyes locked, and Tim extended his left palm, slowly making contact in a perfect fit.

"*Quien eres?*" the stranger asked, his eyes riveted on Tim.

It was then that Tim made the connection: he was the policeman Tim had noticed staring at him at Recoleta; he was the person whose reflection Tim had seen in the display case in the San Telmo antique shop.

"Who are you?" the stranger repeated in English. "I've been watching you."

"I know," Tim stammered.

"I should be stoned," his double said, still fixated on Tim. "This is unreal. It's fucking unreal. Who the fuck are you?"

"I'm Tim."

"American? A tourist?"

"Yes."

"I'm Jeff," the young man said, extending his hand.

"Your name really is Jeff?" Tim asked in disbelief.

"Yes, anything wrong with that?"

"No. Nothing at all. I just knew someone …"

The pair stood in front of Guido's shoe emporium, the damp night mist creating a light fog around the two figures.

"You look cold," Jeff said, moving a step closer to Tim. "Want to go somewhere?"

"Sure," Tim said, hesitant but fascinated.

"I'm only a few blocks away on Maipu." Jeff put an arm across Tim's shoulder and pressed him close. "You are something else!"

The apartment was minimalist, with hardly any furniture, but it had a commanding view of the Plaza de la Republica on Avenida 9 de

Julio in the distance. Tim was looking out at *El Obelisco*, the obelisk in the center of the square, standing like a proud shaft illuminated in the foggy night, as his host came up from behind and placed an open beer in his hand.

"Don't talk," Jeff said, removing Tim's leather jacket and pushing up his T-shirt. "I'm not, you know, into guys, but this is different."

Tim put the beer down and slowly slid Jeff's shirt up over his head. They stood bare-chested, hands exploring each other's exposed torsos, tracing bodies that were identical, even to the V-shaped patches of hair that disappeared below their belt buckles. Their jeans dropped to the floor like fallen drapes, Jockey shorts tangled clumsily around their ankles, as the two stood naked, connected by probing tongues in an impassioned kiss neither understood.

Hazy morning light streamed in through the open sliding glass doors of the small terrace off the apartment. Tim slid his hand over the sleeping body on the floor next to him, gently cupping Jeff's rounded cheeks, which clenched involuntarily in half-sleep.

"Want coffee?" Jeff asked through squinting eyes, sitting up with a full erection.

"I should be going," Tim said, not moving but also fully aroused.

The two embraced and rolled across the floor, hugging each other so tightly, they could have melted their two bodies into one. Their lovemaking was savage and severe, each desperately trying to devour the other.

"You know, I'm not queer," Jeff said, standing up naked, gasping from the passionate encounter. "But seeing you …" He stopped, kissing Tim on the lips.

Tim pulled back gently, looking at his double. "When is your birthday?"

"Why? Going to send me a present?" Jeff smiled softly.

"No. I was just curious."

"July," Jeff answered. "Twenty-first."

"Mine's the twentieth," Tim announced, looking at Jeff.

"We could almost be twins," Jeff laughed, not comprehending the impact his suggestion had on Tim.

"Almost ..." Tim said wistfully, looking out the sliding glass doors to the Plaza de la Republica three blocks away. "I'd better be going. I'm traveling with my aunt, who will be wondering where I am." Tim looked at his watch. "Christ, it's after ten o'clock," he said, alarmed.

"Can we get together later?" Jeff asked. "I have class this afternoon, but I'm off tonight."

"Are you in school?" Tim asked.

"More like training," Jeff answered evasively. "I work nights as a bartender at the Sheraton Hotel, but I'm off tonight. It would be fun to show you the real Buenos Aires, not where tourists hang out."

"I'd like that," Tim responded.

"Call me later," Jeff said, handing Tim a sheet of Sheraton stationery with his phone number and name printed neatly in block letters: Jeffrey Martinez. Then, placing both hands on Tim's shoulders, Jeff kissed his double gently on the lips. "You are something."

"I'll call you," Tim said, slipping out of the apartment to the elevator down the hallway. Out in the bright sunshine on Maipu, he walked the few blocks back to the Claridge in a daze, wondering whether he had been hallucinating or had actually met his double.

Blade was sitting in the paneled dining room off the lobby, sipping coffee and reading the *International Herald Tribune*. News of the war in the Middle East was troubling.

"Good morning." Tim kissed his aunt on the cheek and pulled up a chair to join her. "I hope you weren't worried."

"No, I wasn't worried." Blade looked up from the paper to inspect her nephew. "You know I don't keep tabs on you."

"Coffee, Mr. Halladay?" the waiter asked.

"Yes, please."

"Perhaps you should have a drink," Blade suggested half-jokingly.

"A bit early, even for me," Tim returned.

The two sat at the table in silence, absorbed in very different thoughts. They were the only guests in the dining room. Blade broke the silence by sliding a yellow envelope across the starched white linen tablecloth. "Here, you need to read this."

Tim looked at his aunt and then took the Western Union envelope in his hand and opened it. The terse message from his father would change his life forever:

> *Received notification from U.S. Army. Tim to report for involuntary induction into Army at New Haven headquarters on Monday, July 10. Suggest cutting trip short and return home.*

Tim stared at the telegram and then reread it. Blade was silent, for once not knowing what to say. Crumpling the Western Union paper in his hand, Tim threw it across the table. "Shit!"

"I know. It's terrible," Blade said sympathetically.

"This fucks up everything," Tim spit angrily. "Sorry, but everything is just fucked."

"I know, Tim. It's very unfair." After pausing a minute, she said, "You know you could always ..."

Tim cut her off. "Always what? Check the box?" he cried out. "Never. Don't even go there."

"Well, a lot of boys do it, whether they are or not."

"Forget it. I don't even want to talk about it."

Blade backed off, sensing this was an option her nephew had already firmly rejected.

"I've rebooked our flight to leave tomorrow," Blade announced. "We're on the midnight PanAm flight to New York. I've arranged to have a car pick us up at Kennedy and drive us to Georgetown."

"What about Iguazu Falls?"

"I've canceled. It's more important we get home right now. Besides, the weather at Iguazu has been bad—rain every day—so we'll just have to do that next time," Blade said, trying to put a positive spin on the situation.

Back in the suite, Tim took a long shower and then stretched out naked on the bed. He tried to sleep, but his head was spinning; his whole world had changed in the last twenty-four hours. Blade had made an excuse to leave the suite, saying she wanted to have a massage and manicure, to allow her nephew private time to himself that afternoon. Tim dressed, putting on the same clothes from the night before, and walked out the porte cochere of the Claridge, heading down Tucuman in the cool but sunny autumn afternoon. It was early lunchtime in Buenos Aires, and the streets were busy. He crossed Maipu where he'd left Jeffrey Martinez's apartment a few hours earlier. The doorman at Jeffrey's building looked at him but said nothing. Tim turned right on Florida and paused in front of Guido's shoe emporium, looking into the display windows filled with elegant leather goods. He hesitated, contemplating whether he should inquire about whether his wing tips were ready, but decided to move on. Two blocks later, he crossed bustling Avenida Corrientes, jammed with taxis and well-dressed *porteños* out for the midday break. The oversized painted billboard of tango legend Carlos Gardel, dressed in top hat and black formal attire, leaning on an elegant walking cane, loomed over *Los Inmortales*, the famous pizzeria named for the many writers, actors, singers, and musicians who had frequented the restaurant.

Upon entering the restaurant through the revolving front door, Tim was greeted by the maître d' in a black suit and ushered to a table draped in a crisp white linen cloth. From the wood-paneled wall of the restaurant, scores of framed black-and-white photos signed by artists and celebrities peered out over the room. A wooden ceiling fan whirled quietly overhead, spreading the aroma of garlic and onions cooking in olive oil. Tim was handed a menu by a waiter dressed in a starched white shirt and tight black pants.

"Welcome to *Los Inmortales*," he said in English, placing a basket of breadsticks on the table as he poured Tim a small glass of champagne. The menu listed over fifty different pizzas with a selection of toppings—artichokes, seafood, asparagus, grilled vegetables, chicken, salami, cheeses—and a choice of crusts, from crispy thin (*a la piedra*) to thick and spongy (*de molde*). Tim ordered the thin crust with mushrooms and a half-carafe of house red wine.

After refilling the glass of complimentary champagne, the waiter brought Tim's order. He unfolded a fresh white napkin and, brushing up against the side of the table, asked, "Can I get you anything else?"

A woman sitting across from Tim squashed a cigarette into an ashtray on the adjoining table and blew a cloud of smoke into the air. She winked seductively and then pushed her chair back to leave. Tim turned the other way, wishing he smoked or knew how to say something clever in Spanish. He finished the last slice of pizza, washing it down with the cheap red wine that was now giving him a glow. It was the first food he'd had since dinner with Blade the night before. He paid the check and headed back out to bustling Corrientes, crossing the Plaza de la Republica with its huge limestone obelisk rising in the center. Wailing sirens pierced the afternoon air, and the shrill honking of police horns forced people to put fingers to their ears. Tim saw a commotion in the next block behind the Colon Theatre. As he drew closer, he saw riot police with batons drawn racing down the alleyway, converging on Café Einstein. Wooden wine barrels that had served as makeshift tables the night before were splintered into pieces on the street, and candle-dripped beer and wine bottles were smashed into a pile of debris as the khaki-uniformed police stormed the small after-hours club. The blond folk singer who only hours earlier had been singing "We Shall Overcome" was in handcuffs, shoved into the back of a police van, his guitar smashed and thrown into the heap of rubble on the street. Tim had been warned by M that the Argentine government, under the military dictatorship of Juan Carlos Onganía, was harassing liberal students and intellectuals. The harassment had erupted the year before, only a month after Onganía assumed power, in *La Noche de los Bastones Largos* (the Night of the Long Police Batons), a landmark confrontation between the military police and students and faculty at the University of Buenos Aires. It was an attack on any form of liberal or avant-garde thinking. This repressive environment was the driving force that had led M to leave Argentina and continue his education at Georgetown.

As he drew closer to the now burning pile of rubble in the alley, Tim could see the riot police, helmets strapped under their chins, batons drawn, smashing bottles. None of them could have been older than Tim. One was urinating on the smoldering heap of trash, laughing. Tim's eyes focused on the young riot policeman buttoning up his trousers, his back toward him. *Is this what military service was going to do to him?* Then it registered. The laughing, pissing policeman was Jeffrey—his double. So this is what Jeff meant when he said he was in training. Tim was enraged, disgusted. He turned and walked in a trance against the throngs of people pushing to see what the disturbance in the alleyway was all about.

At the Claridge, Tim passed the doorman without speaking, retrieved his key from the front desk, and let himself into the suite. He stripped out of his clothes, slipped on the plush terry robe hanging on the back of the bathroom door, and then went into the sitting room to fix a drink. The door to Blade's room was closed, but he could hear her talking on the phone. The shoebox from Guido's emporium was sitting outside his room. Tim opened the package to examine the custom brown leather wing tips, wondering when and where he would have an occasion to wear them.

Tim picked up the sheet of Sheraton stationery with Jeff's name and phone number and looked at it, wondering whether a real person had written on the paper. Then he took a ballpoint pen from the desk and drew the eerie arches and almond-shaped eyes on top of the letterhead, bearing down hard on the desk, carving deep gashes into the wooden surface on which the paper rested. Tears flowed down his cheeks as he wrote forcefully, "Jeffrey Wasn't Here." He took the paper into the bathroom and stared at himself in the mirror. He looked at Jeffrey for the last time and ignited the paper with a match. The flame shot up in front of the mirror, and he let the paper fall into a curl in the marble sink. Tim turned on the faucet to wash the flaky gray ashes down the drain. He would not see Jeff again; he would not call him. Tim wanted the memory of his double to be just that—maybe a fantasy, maybe a hallucination. He wanted to wipe the image of the laughing, pissing riot policeman from his mind, but he knew it would always be there, somewhere. He prayed his fixation with his twin brother had disappeared with the burnt ashes of the Sheraton Hotel letterhead, but he could not be sure. He did know there would be no more Kilroy graffiti.

The PanAm flight back to New York was not as festive as the Varig trip down to Rio. Tim had two strong scotches, declined the fancy dinner service, and went to sleep in the window seat opposite Blade, pulling a blanket up over his head. He was awakened from the alcohol-induced escape by a gentle tap on his shoulder from a flight attendant in the familiar blue uniform, asking if he would like breakfast.

"We'll be landing at Kennedy in about an hour," she advised.

"Just coffee and juice," Tim answered sleepily, returning his seat to an upright position.

"You were exhausted," Blade said, stroking Tim softly on his arm. "I let you sleep."

"I'm fine," Tim said, sitting up.

Blade charmed her way through customs, whisking the vicuña fur and the half-passenger/half-military ship model past the inspectors as though the items were cheap souvenirs purchased last-minute at an airport gift shop. Tim suspected that someone had already been alerted, but he said nothing. The drive down the New Jersey Turnpike to DC was monotonous, and they arrived at Thirty-Third Street just after one in the afternoon. The townhouse was empty, but Mattie had left a note on the kitchen table welcoming Blade and Tim back from their trip and advising them that she had prepared a chicken salad and tomato aspic, now chilling in the refrigerator.

Tim opened his suitcase on the bed in the downstairs apartment, taking out only his shaving kit and toiletries. He would be packing up again in a few days to go to his parents' home in Westport and to report for his induction into the army in New Haven.

Tim went into the greenhouse to find two pots of Paperwhite Narcissus that Duane had moved to a sunny spot. The forced bulbs were in full bloom. With a pair of garden shears he clipped the delicate flowers from each container. He wrapped a bouquet of two dozen stems in newspaper and slipped out the back gate to his battered VW parked in the alley.

Tim drove across Key Bridge to Arlington Cemetery. He pulled over on the gravel road on the hillside not far from the JFK eternal flame memorial and retraced his steps from six months earlier. He easily found Red's grave and knelt at the site, releasing the bouquet from its newspaper wrapping and spread the flowers on the damp grass. He embraced the cold stone marker and pressed his cheek against the etched engraving of Red's name. The delicate white narcissus blossoms looked up at him like innocent, questioning cupids.

EPILOGUE

The year was 1967. Young men were burning their draft cards and refusing to cut their long hair, using the excuse they were in a rock band. Some were planning to move to Canada, ready to embrace a maple leaf before dying for stars and stripes. Straight men were "checking the box," choosing to lie about sucking cock rather than die for a war they knew nothing about and had no passion for. Their homes, moms, and girlfriends were not being threatened by men with slanty eyes, so why did they have to go halfway around the world to kill them? The Vietnam War, in media terms only a conflict, was wiping their high school buddies off the street. Images of naked children running down dirt roads, arms open and burned beyond recognition, looking like maple syrup had been poured over their bodies, were on the front page of the *Daily News*—proof that the napalm sprayed into the palm-tree jungles was effective.

The Arab-Israeli War, later to be dubbed the Six-Day War, lasted from June 5 to June 10, 1967. The international tension escalated the draft movement in the United States. Tim was caught up in the wave of hysteria, and instead of reporting to Yale Drama School on Chapel Street in New Haven, he checked into the US Army Recruitment Center at 129 Church Street on July 10, 1967. Even Tim saw the ironic humor of ending up in church rather than chapel, but the humor quickly subsided as he stood in line in his Jockey shorts, behind the beefy black and Puerto Rican boys from Bridgeport, his clothes in a plastic bag in his hand, waiting to report for his interview with the army doctor who would ask the question about his tendencies. He had no idea that his denial would eventually place him in escape and evasion exercises at Fort Lee, Virginia, preparing him to become a tunnel rat.

Tim's dad had driven the Lincoln up Merrit Parkway to New Haven that July morning on the way to the Army Recruitment Center, as Lulu sang "To Sir with Love" over the car radio. As they pulled up to the dingy brick government building on Church Street, Tim opened the car door, gathered his duffel bag, and started to leave.

"Good luck, son," his dad said, extending a hand. "Be careful."

"Sure, Dad," Tim said, holding his father's hand tightly. "You know I will."

The big Lincoln edged away from the curb, and as Tim waved, the sounds of the Beatles' latest hit song, "All You Need Is Love," faded from the car radio into the muggy July morning air.

CPSIA information can be obtained at www.ICGtesting.com
Printed in the USA
BVOW04s1927041114

373663BV00002B/13/P